The
Heart-Stirring
Sermon

and other stories

the HEART-STIRRING SERMON

AND OTHER STORIES

AVRAHAM REISEN

Edited, Translated, and
with an Introduction
and Annotations by
Curt Leviant

THE OVERLOOK PRESS
Woodstock, New York

First published in 1992 by
The Overlook Press
Lewis Hollow Road
Woodstock, New York 12498

This work was supported by a grant from the National Endowment
for the Humanities.

Library of Congress Cataloging-in-Publication Data

Reisen, Abraham, 1876-1953
   [Short stories. English. Selections]
   The heart-stirring sermon: stories/ by Avraham Reisen
translated from the Yiddish and edited by Curt Leviant.
   p.   cm.
   1. Reisen, Abraham, 1876-1953—Translations into English.
I. Leviant, Curt. II. Title.

PJ5129.R37A26   1992
839'.0933—dc20   91-26799
                                                      CIP

ISBN 0-87951-436-1

Designed by Hannah Lerner
Printed in the United States of America

ACKNOWLEDGMENTS

Special appreciation is tendered to the following for kindly explaining rare words or phrases, especially of Slavic origin, in the Reisen text:

Dina Abramowicz, Mikhl Baran, Dr. Jacob Halberstam, Joseph Mlotek, and Dr. Mordkhe Schaechter.

And many thanks to Frances Hoffman for assiduously typing and retyping the manuscript and for making valuable suggestions

For
Dalya and Harry, Dvora and David, Shulamit and Ira
and for
Leora
with hopes that she
will read Reisen someday in the
original

A bouquet of thanks to the Reisen family,
whose generosity helped in the publication of this book

CONTENTS

INTRODUCTION

AVRAHAM REISEN (1876–1953) was born in Kaidanov, near Minsk, in White Russia, to a family that valued writing: his father, Kalman, was a merchant who wrote poetry; his brother, Zalman, became a noted literary historian; and his sister, Sarah, was a poet too. Apart from receiving a very thorough and traditional Jewish education, Reisen was also tutored privately in Russian, German, and other secular subjects.

In his late teens he was already corresponding with Sholom Aleichem and sending him poems for publication. In one letter, Sholom Aleichem (1859–1916) praised the young poet and promised a surprise that would please him. The great Yiddish humorist had sent several of Reisen's poems to a Yiddish newspaper in Philadelphia with the recommendation that they be published. Soon an envelope with a United States postmark came and the young Reisen read his first work published in America. Crowning the surprise was a tribute by Sholom Aleichem himself; in a postscript to the poems, he compared the talented teenager to a contemporary of his, the great Yiddish poet Shimon Frug.

During this period Reisen was also exchanging letters with I. L. Peretz (1851–1915); he too encouraged the young writer and admired his work. Meanwhile, Reisen continued his self-education by reading widely in European literature, and when he was drafted into the czar's army, he became acquainted with the works of Chekhov.

After his induction Reisen quickly learned to play the baritone horn, which enabled him to become a member of the regimental band. This assignment eased what would have normally been an arduous tour of duty, especially for a Jew in the Russian army. A story connected with his service may be paradigmatic of Reisen's character. One day a civilian friend advised Reisen not to waste

the best years of his life in uniform and offered to help him flee
to the United States. Reisen declined. The desertion of a Jewish
soldier would not only create a bad impression, he explained, but
would make the other Jewish soldiers in the regiment suffer.

In the late 1890s, after his discharge from the army, Reisen
was a private tutor for a while, a common occupation for young
Jewish intellectuals at the time (foremost among them: Sholom
Aleichem and the Hebrew national poet Chaim Nachman Bialik).
Reisen then moved to Warsaw, where he befriended his mentor
and literary counselor, I. L. Peretz. It was at this time that Reisen
began publishing the short stories that later appeared in his first
book of prose, in 1903. Restless and energetic, he wandered from
city to city, intermittently working on a number of periodicals
and journals. By 1908, when his first collected works of poetry
and fiction appeared, Reisen had become famous wherever Yiddish
was spoken and read.

By now it was the turn of other young writers to seek *him* out.
That same year the aspiring young Hebrew writer S. Y. Agnon
— who was to win the Nobel Prize for Literature in 1966 — was
about to make *aliya* to the Land of Israel from his home in Galicia,
Poland. Yosef Chaim Brenner, the noted Hebrew writer, had given
Agnon a letter of introduction to Reisen in Cracow. During the
visit, Reisen gave the twenty-year-old Agnon a book of his
poems, and in turn Agnon read Reisen a Yiddish short story he
had written. (Although he would achieve fame as a Hebrew writer,
Agnon began writing in Yiddish, following a tradition begun in
the middle of the nineteenth century, when many of the leading
Jewish writers in Eastern Europe — Peretz, Mendele, Sholom
Aleichem — were creating works in both Hebrew and Yiddish).
Reisen immediately accepted Agnon's story but soon lost the
manuscript.

Several years later, before the outbreak of World War I, both
writers met in a café in Berlin. Between coffee and cognac, Agnon
recalls in a memoir, Reisen told him to fetch pencil and paper and

jot down the contents of his Yiddish story and some of the expressions he remembered. Agnon, however, never got a chance to write anything, for Reisen was in high spirits, engaged in a world of his own. He had just gotten payment for one of his own stories, Agnon recalls, and had ordered the café's musicians to play a Jewish tune for everyone's entertainment.

In 1914 Reisen settled in the United States and for the next four decades lived in New York, where, like many other Yiddish writers, he was associated with various Yiddish dailies — *Der Tog, Di Freiheit*, and the *Forverts* (The Jewish Daily Forward) —publishing a story each week. In 1917 a twelve-volume edition of his poems and stories was published. But Reisen's literary activity was not limited to fiction and poetry. He was also a playwright (many of his one-act plays were staged), memoirist, essayist, literary critic, editor, publisher, and translator, responsible for bringing many works into Yiddish, including Heine's German and Bialik's Hebrew poetry.

That Reisen was influenced by Chekhov's manner, style, and poignant characterization is apparent even from a cursory reading of his stories: note Reisen's focus on people of humble origins, downtrodden by the exigencies of life. Reisen is not, however, a slavish imitator of the great Russian master, nor could he be if he wished, for the cultural nexus is entirely different. Reisen portrays a Jewish society whose Jewishness is not merely skin-deep but an all-encompassing element of daily life. Indeed, in his stories, Reisen makes rich and subtle use of the mainstream of Jewish religious culture, a literary usable past that enriches the literature of any nation.

Reisen also quotes and transmutes liturgy, the Midrash and the Talmud, the Bible and other texts, as well as signs and symbols from Jewish life, thought, and values. With the nearly four thousand years of Jewish civilization, memories, and traditions to draw from, any writer composing in Hebrew or Yiddish has an abundance of material, and Reisen was fully aware of these literary treasures.

Avraham Reisen was also well versed in the literary traditions of the West. He read German and Russian literature in the original and works from other languages in translation, and he himself translated Japanese and Persian poetry (from a German version) into Yiddish. Like many nineteenth-century Jewish autodidacts, Reisen was a sophisticated reader who skillfully blended a Western sensibility with the millennia-old traditions of the Jews in his writing.

Despite this link to a specific culture, Reisen is neither abstruse or inaccessible. His people are recognizable; their emotions and problems leap the gap of cultural boundaries. Perhaps the most impressive evidence of Reisen's universal appeal is his translation into so many languages: his stories appeared in newspapers and magazines in English, Russian, German, Polish, Spanish, Hungarian, Romanian, Italian, Bulgarian, Latvian, and Danish. As if to demonstrate the universality of Reisen's appeal — despite his focus on East European Jewish life — the noted Danish literary critic Georg Brandes (himself a Jew) singled out Reisen as a Yiddish writer of extraordinary originality and scope.

It is this close, almost seamless interlinking of Western aesthetics with the rich lodestone of Jewish lore and literary tradition that makes Avraham Reisen a modern master of the Yiddish short story. Fortunately, recognition came to him early. The first few years of the twentieth century, critics in New York (1902), Cracow (1903), and London (1904) were already evaluating Reisen's contribution to Yiddish literature, and the stream of attention never ceased. In Yiddish alone, some six hundred articles, reviews, and essays have been devoted to Reisen's works.

Although his stories and poems were often included in English anthologies of Yiddish and general Jewish literature (even as early as 1912), this volume represents the first book in English devoted solely to Avraham Reisen's fiction.

During a career that spanned more than five decades, Reisen focused on three major themes. The first is the shtetl where Jews are rooted in their society. This was Reisen's domain: the life of the poor, unsophisticated Jews of Eastern Europe, children and adults, workers and petty merchants — and the qualities of *mentchlichkeyt* (decency) inherent in them, as seen in "The Heart-Stirring Sermon," "Too Late," and "The Poor Community." But Reisen doesn't view Jewish life through nostalgic lenses, nor does he create apologia. "Shut In" and "Matza for the Rich" dispel the illusion that *mentchlichkeyt* is universally practiced in the shtetl.

A second major theme is the life of the young Jewish intellectual away from home. In these stories, the hero often attempts to earn a livelihood in new surroundings, and Reisen conveys the hero's internal alienation, his self-imposed exile, his struggles for independence and dignity. In "The Counterfeit Coin," for example, an unemployed tutor in a big town tries to buy some groceries with a false coin. Soon the starving but sensitive young man is conscience-stricken by his deception and cannot make a purchase.

In the third category of tales, Reisen depicts the immigrant experience and shows how America changes the Old World Jew. The conflict between the veteran New Yorker and the greenhorn is an ongoing one. A brother-in-law in "Rockefeller and Rothschild" continually pokes fun at his newcomer relative until one day the latter decides to stand his ground. The Old World rabbi of "New Bosses" quickly learns that the men who were considered unlearned louts in the shtetl are now the trustees of his New York synagogue. If he wants to hold on to his job, the rabbi must accommodate himself to their desire for snappier and less scholarly sermons.

Reisen's hallmark — compassion — surfaces in all his stories. "Lost His Voice" describes a cantor who fears he can no longer sing, while "Too Late" focuses on a poor gentile peasant who sells

xvi AVRAHAM REISEN

his pine cuttings to the Jews for Sukkos every year. One year, when the peasant arrives a day late, the local Jews commiserate and unite to help him. And Reisen's special empathy for children is seen in "Reisele," "Shut In," and "When Does Mama Eat?," in which the bittersweet pains of childhood recall Chekhov's touching tale "Vanka."*

Reisen has particularly good insights into poverty's stressful psychological effects. The needy hero in "The Free Loan" finally gathers his courage to go to a rich acquaintance up the street, but pride prevents him from admitting his true financial straits. And Grunem, the impoverished teacher of "A Pinch of Snuff" has prayed in the same shul for fifteen years with the shtetl's richest man but has never dared speak to him. When the poor teacher finally does approach him, an unfortunate mishap dashes his hope for salvation.

Along with Grunem, Reisen's other heroes are almost uniformly frustrated: poverty, a lack of decisiveness and self-confidence, fear of the rich, interpersonal strife, the economic system all combine to stymie Reisen's Jews. Most are constantly struggling to survive — but life collapses in on them like a black hole, for that is the reality of Jewish life in Eastern Europe.

In only one instance was Reisen remiss in compassion for a protagonist. After Peretz had read "Avraham the Shoemaker" he told Reisen that he had treated his hero too cruelly. Only years later, Reisen admits in his memoirs, did he realize how right Peretz was. Reisen contends, however, that "Avraham the Shoemaker," whose eponymous hero makes his meager living patching shoes damaged by the perennial autumnal mud, was a symbolic story about those who live in, and by, mud. Nevertheless, without this authorial intervention, the reader would be hard put to

*In "Vanka," a nine-year-old orphan boy, apprenticed to a shoemaker for three months, is abused by his master, ill-fed, and harassed. He writes a letter to his grandfather, pleading that he take him home. But the only address the lad writes on the envelope besides his name is "To Grandfather in the Village." And thus he posts it in the mailbox.

consider this a symbolic narrative. In fact, no tales in Reisen's realistic *oeuvre* have symbolic underpinning.

In all of Reisen's fiction traditional Jewish values are highlighted: compassion for the poor; love of tradition, books, and learning; social justice; tenderness between parents and children. But in spite of the abundance of all other kinds of love, only one kind is noticeably missing: that between husband and wife.

Not only is affection absent in many of the stories where couples appear but disdain seems to prevail. A kind word is seldom heard between husband and wife. "A Woman's Fear," for instance, begins with Chiyeneh's desire to cook something new to please her husband; but we soon learn that he has long been the cause of her weeping. Chiyeneh fears getting the glasses she badly needs lest her husband leave her. Similarly, in some of the other tales where husband and wife converse, the man is gruff, mocking, and sarcastic. (In "Lost His Voice," however, it is the wife who takes the nasty initiative.) Although Jewish tradition mandates that a husband respect his wife, in many stories the wife is at best tolerated, with impatience and occasional rage.

The frustrations of poverty may be one cause of this sandpaper attitude, but it may also be understood in the context of education. Learning was highly esteemed, but only boys had the obligation to study; they became experts in the sacred Hebrew texts, while girls remained relatively ignorant (they were taught only to read Hebrew and Yiddish). The woman was excluded from advanced learning because it was her responsibility to manage the household and care for the children. At the same time, she was thought to be of a lower social stature for she wasn't on an intellectual par with the men — a no-win situation. Even in the World to Come, it was believed, men would sit on a comfortable chair in the Garden of Eden, while wives would serve as their footstools. It should be mentioned, however, that there are always exceptions to the general belief. For instance, in a memorable short tale, "Idyllic Home," I. L. Peretz has his hero lovingly tell his wife,

"I don't want you to be my footstool. I will bend down to you and we will sit on one chair."

Nevertheless, despite all this, it was the woman who first inculcated the children with the values of *Yiddishkeyt* that would shape them the rest of their lives. Long before the child began school (at age four or five), it was from the mother that he heard Biblical tales and legends and the accompanying ethical and moral subtexts.

Although both Sholom Aleichem and Reisen wrote about the poor, the lines of influence between the humorist and Reisen are rather tenuous. Sholom Aleichem approached Jewish life, and indeed the Yiddish language, basically through the medium of humor (though the plaintive, anguished streak indeed is present: witness the Tevye stories, which, despite the patina of comedy, are intrinsically tragic). Sholom Aleichem also told his stories in various voices: monologue, first-person narrator, and omniscient author. Avraham Reisen, presumably so preoccupied with the awful straits that many of his characters are in, has little humor in his work and almost no playfulness in his use of Yiddish. Sholom Aleichem, like Reisen, drew from the surrounding Jewish world, but he also utilized the oral tradition: jokes, Hasidic anecdotes, and tales, which he fleshed out into full-fledged stories. Sholom Aleichem too was more open to the tangentially absurd ("The Clock That Struck Thirteen") and even the borderline macabre ("Eternal Life," where a man has to find a burial place in midwinter for his wife, who has just died).

Reisen speaks only in the omniscient author's voice, and each of his tales encapsulates the truth of daily life. There is no comic, or even tragic, exaggeration, no social satire. Since Reisen was an early socialist, it is to this ideology that one might turn for one of the influences upon his work. Reisen wanted desperately to call the public's attention to the plight of the poor, the miserable, the hopeless. And so, time and again, in many of his stories,

impoverished Jews are thrust center stage. It is a determined social
conscience, nurtured by both the Jewish tradition of compassion
and the socialist's ideal of humaneness, that informs Reisen's
work. To a degree, Reisen's style and narrative manner are perhaps
prisoners of his social philosophy. Sholom Aleichem, on the other
hand, was an adherent of no party and no political philosophy,
and thus was able to write from various perspectives. (Uniquely,
at a fiftieth-anniversary banquet in his honor, Jews of all economic,
political, and religious persuasions, secular and pious, Zionist and
non-Zionist, banded together for a wall-to-wall committee to pay
Sholom Aleichem tribute.)

From the early classic Yiddish writers, especially I. L. Peretz,
Reisen drew sustenance, learning how to include Jewish themes
and images subtly in his fiction; but it is from his older Russian
contemporary, Chekhov, that Reisen derives the substance of his
style and approach to fiction — indeed, the Chekhovian voice
that he melded with his Jewish ethos for the rest of his career.

Not that Chekhov taught Reisen about compassion. Sympathy
for one's character is a hallmark of Yiddish literature — Sholom
Aleichem and Peretz abound with it. But Chekhov taught Reisen
how to take a character and have him move to the forefront of
the reader's consciousness through the character's thoughts and
actions. Take, for example, the story "Shut In," which is told from
the point of view of a little boy who is constantly harassed by his
father. The lad's desire for a bit of freedom — some breathing
space, some fresh air, some fun — is constantly suppressed by
the strict, insensitive father. In "The Last Hope" a man desperately
needs a loan and plans to approach the local rich man. But like
money in the bank, he saves it for when he will need it more.

Reisen achieved his effects with a superb economy of means.
Like Chekhov, Reisen has that inimitable quality of depicting
ordinary people's hopes and anguish in simple language that
speaks directly to their hearts. Yet his sympathy for his characters

does not impinge upon his objectivity. Like the Russian master he blends intimacy and distance superbly.

Understandably, Reisen's fiction was no clone of either Chekhov's or Peretz's work. One cannot fault a writer for not being like his mentor. A good mentor is delighted — as indeed Peretz was —when his disciple goes his own way. For instance, where Peretz's and Chekhov's comic monologues have that extra dimension, the leap out of the real, Reisen is more direct. His artistic credo is simplicity: the recreation of human beings, their problems, hopes, and fears sans adornment. The anguish of Reisen's protagonists is palpable; no layers of irony or symbolism intrude.

For Sholom Aleichem, art is a transposition of reality: bent, mocked, stretched, compressed. For the Chekhov that Reisen emulated, and for Reisen himself, art is a mirror of reality: life is seen through a frame that defines the art and sharpens the focus. Neither Chekhov nor Reisen judge or moralize; both photograph reality and let the reader draw his own conclusions.

In one of his essays, the noted British critic and short story writer V. S. Pritchett correctly observes that "Sholom Aleichem has the style of a spontaneous talker." Indeed, the spirals of narration are omnipresent in his monologues, often told in roundabout fashion: two steps forward, one step back. The narrator holds cards that he reveals later, or not at all. Occasionally, there is even no ending to a story, as in "Sixty-six," where the central speaker, spinning a yarn in a moving train, simply gets out at his station at the crux of the story.

But in Avraham Reisen there is relentless forward movement. Plot and time are kinetic. Memory, flashbacks, play minor roles; they are interwoven into an occasional paragraph for the sake of clarification (as in "Reisele" or "A Woman's Fear"), but they don't play an integral role in the story's structure.

One trait that distinguishes Reisen from the great Yiddish humorist is that in his stories laughter doesn't countervail the tears. For Reisen zeroes in on real life and its anxieties. In "Leap Year" a woman baking bread for a living (her husband has long been unemployed) goes to a neighbor's house to borrow an oven shovel. But too polite to ask straight out for the needed item, she gets involved in a long discussion with her neighbors about the Jewish calendar; by the time she comes home her earnings have gone up in smoke.

The Yiddish-speaking world crossed national boundaries and even conflicting political systems: Poland, Russia, Romania, Austro-Hungary, Czechoslavakia, South Africa, Argentina, Mexico, and other South American countries, as well as enclaves in Paris and Berlin, and of course the United States and England. In all of these places, Avraham Reisen was as popular and critical a success as the three founding fathers of modern Yiddish literature, Mendele Mocher Seforim, I. L. Peretz, and Sholom Aleichem.

Reisen's poems and short stories were avidly read and he was held in high esteem by his reading public as well as by literary critics. His verses, reflecting the same themes as his fiction, were often set to music; sung by thousands of people, they achieved the status of folk songs and were internationally popular. When he visited his homeland — by then the Soviet Union — in 1928, thousands of admirers in each city turned out to greet the man who had become a legend in his own lifetime. No other Yiddish writer besides Sholom Aleichem had received such an outpouring of love and esteem.

Perhaps the finest assessment of Reisen's place in modern Yiddish literature comes from the critic Ben Zion Goldberg, whose remark is quoted in the *Lexicon of Yiddish Literature*: "After the great classical triumvirate of Mendele, Peretz, and Sholom Aleichem, Reisen is the fourth. He is the first of the new generation of Yiddish writers, both in popularity and in the people's affection."

This praise should not be considered lightly, for Goldberg was Sholom Aleichem's son-in-law, and it may be safely said that while familial loyalty is strong, relatives are usually reticent in comparing their kinsman to other writers. Another, more contemporary evaluation of Avraham Reisen may be found in the comprehensive introduction *A Treasury of Yiddish Stories*, edited by Irving Howe and Eliezer Greenberg:

"In the hundreds of stories he wrote . . . Reisen has provided one of the truest and fullest portraits we have of Jewish life in Eastern Europe."

The task of translating Reisen is not a simple one. No translation from the Yiddish may be considered easy, since it involves not only a high level of linguistic mastery but also a deep familiarity with Hebrew (some 15 to 20 percent of Yiddish vocabulary is Hebrew) as well as the entire range of Hebrew/Jewish culture, religion, and literature. In addition to the mundane rendering of vocabulary from one language to another, with Yiddish one must also presume cultural interpretation, which is infinitely more complex. Hence, the translator is confronted with transmitting the nuances of a culture, its very essence, its soul.

In his stories, Reisen frequently makes reference to Jewish customs, to abstruse (and no longer used) prayers, to Aramaic passages from the Talmud, to Biblical, Midrashic, and Talmudic quotations. In some stories Reisen has either the narrator or the protagonist mention religious customs long fallen into desuetude. He makes reference to rabbinic personalities from various periods in Jewish history, to rare religious tomes, and to books and socialist tracts that Jews read in the nineteenth century. Occasionally, he uses German words that will not be found in a Yiddish dictionary but constituted the vocabulary of the region where he lived. At times Reisen even uses an older layer of Yiddish that was utilized by the *techines*, the Yiddish prayers written for women in preceding centuries.

In "Ten Pounds Less," Reisen makes casual reference to a liturgical text used once a year. The man in the story hums a little melody from this prayer, which today is rarely recited in synagogue services. Researching this seemingly innocuous phrase necessitated hunting for old prayerbooks. To us, today, the term is abstruse. But in Reisen's time, and for his audience, the reference was readily understood and completely natural: such infusion of classical material into his fiction is quite common.

Without the requisite knowledge of Hebrew and the mainstream of Jewish tradition, a translator from the Yiddish can easily stumble. Here's an example of a mistake made by a translator of a Reisen story that appeared in an anthology some forty years ago: In a sentence that read: "The townspeople went to spend the holidays with the *yishuvniks*," the translator misinterpreted the word *yishuvniks*. He assumed that *yishuvniks* were yeshiva students. He mixed up the Hebrew word *yishuv*, which means "village," with *yeshiva*, which means "talmudical academy." So instead of the townspeople spending the holidays with untutored and simple Jewish villagers the way Reisen had intended it, the townspeople mistakenly appear to be spending the holidays with Talmudic scholars.

As you read these stories, try the old custom of reading them aloud, which people have enjoyed doing with Sholom Aleichem for generations. Somehow Reisen's characters and their various financial or moral quandaries become more poignant when their stories are read aloud. Perhaps this is so because Reisen is a lyrical poet who may have transferred the musical qualities of his poems, which were often intended to be read aloud or sung, to his stories.

Like Sholom Aleichem's fiction, Reisen's stories too may be said to encompass an entire civilization. He writes about the young and old, the pious and the freethinking, the intellectuals and the artisans. We see Jews at home and at work, in school and at the marketplace. He reveals them to us in shtetls and cities, in Europe and America, in countless settings, through the cycle of the Jewish

year. Reisen portrays a people who are at home in their language
and culture, yet not at home in their world, for they are politically
and economically dispossessed and often deprived of basic rights.
Reading Reisen we see the slow and many-layered spin of Jewish
life that the crush of history has, alas, stopped. What remains
instead are the vibrant stories that continue to speak to us, thanks
to the special ambience that Avraham Reisen has created.

Curt Leviant

Note: Unfamiliar words or terms in Yiddish are listed in the
       Glossary. More specific concepts, books, and Jewish tradi-
       tions are explained in the Annotations.

AVRAHAM
THE SHOEMAKER

AVRAHAM THE SHOEMAKER was a tall, thin old man
with a long beard, even longer earlocks, and a big forehead.
If a stranger had met him returning after morning prayers
with his big tallis bag under his arm he would surely have
thought that he had encountered the town rabbi or a
prosperous townsman. Full of self-esteem and not in the
least ashamed of his trade, Avraham had become proud of
his line of work ever since hearing from an itinerant preacher
that the great Talmudic sage, Rabbi Yochanan, had been a
shoemaker. When shoemaking came up in conversation,
Avraham would passionately silence those who disparaged
it, and he would conclude his fiery remarks with:

"You need more evidence? Just remember that Rabbi
Yochanan too was a shoemaker. He also threaded a needle. . . ."

Sometimes this last phrase would be uttered with a laugh,
which Avraham always regretted immediately. His listeners
might think he was laughing at a Talmudic sage! To prevent
Rabbi Yochanan from being angry at him in the Other
World, Avraham would at once amend his statement.

"But of course he himself didn't thread the needle," he would say. "He hired assistants."

Nevertheless, defending shoemaking and bragging about his colleague Rabbi Yochanan didn't help Avraham very much. He never got the respect he sought. Even the little tailor's shul, usually so very tolerant toward all kinds of workingmen, never honored him with a fitting aliya to the Torah on Sabbath. Only on occasion — and then by mistake — did they give him the next-to-last aliya on a Sabbath, and on Simchas Torah they would let him carry the Torah for the Torah circuit called *Ozer Dalim*, or Helper of the Poor. Not because he was a shoemaker, but because he was half a shoemaker, or a "patcher," as he was called in the shtetl. This meant that he did not make new shoes or boots but merely patched up old ones. In fact, he even boasted that long, long ago he had made new shoes too, but ever since the onset of that wild fashion, those narrow tips, he had stopped completely. He didn't want to make a fool of himself.

But the truth was that as a shoe repairer he had no equal. Even the other shoemakers in town, who usually disparaged one another's work, never dared to find fault in Avraham's repair work. On the other hand, no big fuss was ever made over him in town either. People would even laugh at him whenever the occasion arose, and this hurt his pride. Nevertheless, each year there came a time when he would take his revenge on everyone.

He could hardly wait for that season. He was sure it would come; it must! The Almighty would not change the order of the Six Days of Creation: autumn must come every year and the rains must fall. Avraham knew that in autumn it had to rain, and during his long life he had never seen a year without it. It would create mud in town, great mud puddles that Avraham had to have and for which he prayed to God not only for bread but also for an opportunity to square accounts with the townsfolk who laughed at him.

And when Avraham saw the onset of the cold autumn rains as he sat in his sukka during the holiday, he didn't rush into his house until his wife Peshe called him.

"You lunatic!" the old woman shouted. "Who sits in the sukka in such a downpour? Do you want to be more pious than the rabbi? The rain is going to spoil the soup."

"No matter, no matter." A pleased Avraham calmed her as he came into the house. "Today's rain doesn't scare me. This kind of rain creates mud, silly! Mud . . ."

"Then thank God for the mud!" Peshe answered, making a pious face. She recalled that their entire livelihood was derived from the autumnal mud. Avraham finished the meal in the house, and looked out of the window onto the street. Seeing the ground becoming softer, his heart expanded with joy as he began to recognize the signs of his beloved mud.

But when the sun came out, a deathly fear came over him. It seemed that the sun was set on depriving him of his livelihood. . . . But it didn't shine too long, and soon a cloud covered it and Avraham was happy once more. He began to sing, parodying the children's song:

> "God, God send a rain
> in Avraham the shoemaker's name."

And God acceded to Avraham's prayer — all Sukkos long it poured. Jewish children, upset that their holiday was ruined, couldn't even go out for a little while. Avraham, however, was perfectly delighted. On the street the well-known autumnal mud had already formed. It often happened that women would be stuck in the middle of the street and sometimes they removed their shoes. Small children had to be carried over mud puddles and the men avoided them with all kinds of clever devices.

Now Avraham laughed at the sun. So small a disk in the sky could not possibly dry up such a quantity of mud. And even if no more rain fell, the mud would remain for a couple of months at least. But he was certain that it would rain even more. Avraham had unshakable confidence: in the autumn it must rain! He rested during Sukkos and gathered his strength. He knew that after the holiday he would have to work very late each night; he would be inundated with work.

And indeed, on the morning after Sukkos a tumult invariably overtook his house, which was overrun with people for three months and sometimes even longer. From all over town they brought him shoes. With the abundant mud everyone wanted to make sure his shoes were whole. Besides, in the muddy season shoes tore more readily than during the rest of the year.

Avraham knew quite well that this onslaught sustained him for the entire year. True, he did patchwork even during the dry season, but then he wasn't such a big shot. The higher-class shoemakers who made narrow-tip shoes had no work then and had no qualms about competing with Avraham. That's why he now took advantage of the demand and charged as much as the traffic would bear. He set very high fees and refused to drop the price by even a groschen. He didn't care; even a close neighbor couldn't bargain with him. And when someone tried to get a better price by saying,

"Come on, Reb Avraham, why are you charging so much?"
Avraham answered coldly: "Am I forcing you, God forbid?
If it's not worth it, bring your shoes to Berl the shoemaker.
He's also quite good. After all, he makes those narrow
tips. . . ."

Avraham would utter these last words with an ironic tone,
as if to say: "Berl the shoemaker doesn't always fit your
needs. Sometimes you need me too." Avraham wanted to
be sure that indeed they would need him, so he looked out
the window and became even more obstinate. The entire
street was flooded with a watery mud — one could drown
in it! Oh, how you need me now! Avraham smiled and
didn't even look at the customer who held his shoes and
attempted to bargain the fee down by ten groschen. Avraham
felt that now was the time to square accounts with his
enemies who laughed at him — so he took his revenge with
high prices.

And in this way Avraham the patcher lived until he
became very old. Every year he drew his livelihood from
the shtetl's mud and thanked God for so cleverly creating
the world that at a certain season there had to be mud in
the shtetl and his patchwork was in high demand. That is
the reason why Avraham was so delighted with the mud
— it was perhaps even more enchanting than the poet would
find the blue sea. . . . And when he occasionally walked
through the market buying bits of leather straps in the pelt
shops, he proudly surveyed the mud that inundated the
streets and the market where the wealthiest householders
walked with the skirts of their coats tucked up, muttering,
"Some mud! God save us from it!"

Hearing this, Avraham thought: Of course they don't

like it. They could do without the mud, but they don't care what it means to me.

When a customer complained that the mud made life impossible — praying to God to have mercy and let it be dry — the anger would well up in Avraham. But since he could not give vent to his anger, he charged the man two groschen more per patch, all the while thinking, What nonsense that fellow talks!

Once, in the middle of the summer — it was still a long way off to Avraham's patchwork season — he walked through the market and saw a great heap of stones lying smack in the middle of the marketplace. This puzzled him. What did it mean? He approached a shopkeeper and asked why they needed so many stones.

"So many?" the shopkeeper mimicked him ironically. "You consider this a lot? Just wait till you see ten times as much. A hundred times as much."

"But what will they do with so many stones?" Avraham was even more puzzled.

"Don't you live here?" the shopkeeper said angrily. "Don't you know that very soon they're going to pave the street of this shtetl? First the market, then all the other streets."

"Paving? Paving? What do you mean, paving?" Avraham scratched his neck in disbelief and horror.

"No wonder the Russians say, *Stari yak mali* — an old man is like a child." The shopkeeper smiled. "What's not to understand? They're going to pave the shtetl streets with these stones to get rid of the mud."

Avraham needed no more explanations. The last phrase — "to get rid of the mud" — hit him like a thunderbolt.

But he still didn't fully comprehend. On his way home, he gesticulated and talked to himself like a drunkard. What did they mean, to get rid of the mud? How could the shtetl suddenly be dried up?

Then Avraham recalled that a customer had once told him about big cities, which were completely paved and always dry. He came home confused.

"No more mud!" he muttered. "They don't need me any more."

His wife Peshe didn't understand him; she thought he had gone mad. "What are you shouting about?" the old woman raged. "What mud? You want mud now in the middle of the summer? Don't you have enough of it in autumn?"

"Didn't you hear what I said? Those bandits don't want any mud in the fall either. Do you understand? They want to deprive us of bread in our old age."

"What bandits? What are you babbling about?" Now Peshe became frightened.

Avraham himself didn't know who the bandits were, but the anger burned in him and he quickly said, "They don't like the mud! Understand? They're big aristocrats, that's what they are. They want to follow big city ways, so they decided to pave all the streets. Some nerve they have!"

"This will be the end of us!" Peshe wrung her hands. "We are ruined! How will we make a living now?"

"Go ask them," Avraham answered bitterly. "You think they care about us? You think the whole shtetl brings me shoes to repair after Sukkos just because they feel sorry for me? They'd be delighted, those bandits, if they could do without me."

"But do you really think that their shoes won't be torn any more?" Peshe implored with a trace of hope.

"You goose! Of course their shoes will be torn. They'll tear them on the paving stones too, but not the way they used to. Walking on stone only makes the soles wear away, but in the mud the entire leather becomes rotten, and that's the most important thing for me."

Every day Avraham would go to the market to check on the paving. The wound in Avraham's heart grew along with the increasing pile of stones, and he walked about like a sick man.

Still, he hoped that the paving wouldn't begin so soon. And there was proof. He remembered that when they began to build the bathhouse, they also had brought stones and bricks daily. It had seemed that work would begin any minute, but still it dragged on for quite a few years. And Avraham tried to console himself that the paving would only begin toward the end of his life.

But his hope was in vain.

As he walked through the market one fine morning during that summer, Avraham saw a circle of men. He immediately knew this meant bad news. He pushed his way through the crowd and his hands and legs began trembling. He saw White Russians splitting the stones with powerful sledge-hammer blows that echoed in the air. A group of onlookers watched in delight.

"Now things will be fine," said one.

"Fine isn't the word for it," said another. "We'll be rid of the mud plain and simple."

One man in the circle, a town wag, noticed Avraham.

"You see what they're doing, Reb Avraham?" He began

to poke fun at him. "This is going to hurt your livelihood, you know."

Avraham feigned ignorance. "What's the connection? What connection is there between the paving and my work?"

"A big connection!" The wag didn't stop teasing. "When it's dry our boots won't get torn and you'll have fewer patches to put on."

"So he'll start making new boots," another wag piped up. "But, alas, he can't do that. How could he manage that? Avraham is a born patcher."

"Never mind. He'll learn. He has a big forehead."

Everyone laughed.

Now Avraham couldn't contain himself any longer. Touched to his very core by their teasing, he poured out all his bitterness.

"Loafers! You think you're going to make the world over? May you have aches and pains for as long as that mud is going to stay here. You'll still come to me to repair your rotten boots, but I'll skin you with my prices."

"Hurray!" cried one of the young men in the crowd. The merry group standing by the paving stone was having fun now, and the wag began to shout above the din:

"Reb Avraham, no more mud! There will be no more mud. No more mud! Hurray!"

By autumn the paving was still not completed. The mud was no different that year, but Avraham wasn't fated to enjoy it and earn ten-groschen pieces. The last encounter at the market had affected him badly. For a couple of weeks he walked around feeling ill and then he lay down in bed and died.

The people who were with him as he was expiring recounted with a laugh that his last words were "Bandits, no more mud!"

A year after Avraham's death the paving was completed. Peshe, who had lived to see it, constantly bemoaned her late husband with these words: "Avraham, Avraham! If you would get up now from the grave and see what happened to the mud, you'd die all over again."

THE
HEART-STIRRING SERMON

THE VILLAGE OF K. was fortunate to be visited by
many itinerant preachers. Practically every week, especially
during the winter, a traveling preacher would arrive and
delight the village with four or five sermons. The doors of
the big bes medresh were thickly covered with posters, all
beginning: "Preaching today . . ." The gentile woman who
washed those doors each Passover eve had a hard job, poor
thing, scraping off the dried and hardened glue, which had
been liberally applied with communal funds.

Continuous listening to these preachers had greatly re-
fined and developed the public's taste. A unique talent
surfaced in the village — the critic who, with much skill and
feeling, evaluated the merits of each preacher. These critics
profoundly influenced the rest of the public, and thus it
took extraordinary talent to impress a K. audience. They
weren't even ashamed to find fault with the Skidler and
Vidler preachers who, as was evident from the newspapers,
had achieved great fame. Of the great Liebermann, a
preacher universally praised, they merely observed without

enthusiasm that "he wasn't bad." They had heard better sermons.

Traveling preachers, however, who hiked from town to town, fared pretty badly in K. Sometimes it was only after much difficulty that they succeeded in persuading the shamesh to let them preach. Then, on the very next morning, without a by-your-leave, the same shamesh might bluntly inform a preacher that the public no longer wanted to hear him. In so doing, he would slip a few coins from the collection plate into the preacher's hand, and if the latter had the gall to grimace at the pittance, the shamesh would say: "It's a big village." Meaning "You can go begging from door to door if you like."

Once, however, one of these foot-traveling preachers caused a sensation with his sermon. He arrived on a Monday in mid-January after the morning service and entered the bes medresh without any baggage. Who knew where in town he had left it? The shamesh, experienced with itinerant preachers, saw at once that he wasn't one of the celebrated preachers but only one of the common foot travelers, and didn't even give him a second glance. The preacher followed the shamesh around, humming a sad Talmud melody. He obviously wanted to introduce himself, but waited to be greeted first. But the shamesh nonchalantly went about his tasks: he locked the bookcases, extinguished the lamps, berated a few young yeshiva students for smoking, and continued to ignore the guest. The preacher paced about aimlessly, humming his melody, but finally he could no longer stand it. He quietly approached the shamesh and said faintly, "Sholom aleichem. I'm a preacher."

"Aleichem sholom," the shamesh replied coldly and turned to leave.

But the preacher detained him with a question. "May I preach here?"

"I'll see later," the shamesh said haughtily, "during the afternoon service."

Hearing that there was some hope, the preacher collected himself somewhat and felt more confident.

"You should know that I spoke in Minsk last week and, thank God, they liked me there. I'm not one of those small-time preachers, God forbid."

"If so" — the shamesh's tone was milder now — "then you can preach here. In any case, they'll listen."

Soon a poster was pasted on the door: "Preaching today . . ."

After the afternoon service, congregants from all the little prayerhouses gathered in the big bes medresh.

The preacher went up to the pulpit with a frightened air about him, kissed the curtain of the Holy Ark, leafed through the pages of a little book he carried, and began to sing out with a feeble melody: "Gentlemen! In his Book of Proverbs King Solomon makes the following statement. . . ."

The preacher correctly considered King Solomon a man of great wisdom. Of the quoted verse he posed five difficult questions; to answer them properly he quoted a Midrash, two Aggadas, three remarks by Rabbi Bar Bar Khone, and a passage from *Ye'aros Dvash*. He combined and blended everything, then introduced a parable of an only son who traveled to a land across the sea. On the whole, his sermon was on a high level, and in some places even on a par with those of the finest preachers. But somehow it didn't excite the audience. It was hard to explain the reason; perhaps they disliked the melody of his delivery, perhaps the cut of his beard was at fault. His melody was muted but sufficiently sad, and at times it sank into an authentically Jewish hoarseness. His beard, indeed, was not comely; it wasn't the long beard of a preacher that the public favored. With each passing minute his listeners grew increasingly impatient; their attention strayed and the critics began airing their opinions.

"He's no preacher."

"He's got nothing to say."

"His delivery is poor."

"He has no voice."

"He babbles."

A buzz began in the bes medresh that gradually intensified in volume until it became a commotion A few men who stood by the pulpit withdrew to the back. The seats in the vicinity of the preacher emptied. Soon an entire block of seats was vacant. There was a commotion in the rear; the shamesh rapped for order. . . .

The preacher stood on the pulpit, frightened. The commotion, the thinning out of the audience, the sexton's rapping all made him lose his train of thought; now his speech became confused. He confused David with Solomon, and the Zohar with the Midrash. He quickly corrected himself, but to no avail. It made an even worse impression on the audience, which liked a flawless performance. One by one, people walked out. Those close to the pulpit had already dispersed, others yawned. A trustee whispered so loudly into the shamesh's ear, "It's time for the evening service," that the preacher heard him. . . . Even old Moshe the shopkeeper, who never missed a sermon in his life (he always stood next to the pulpit, staring into the preacher's face, listening for quotes of familiar Biblical verses, which the preacher began but did not complete, for he relied on the public's erudition), yawned into the preacher's face and unwillingly retreated.

The sermon became yet more muddled and incoherent. The preacher stood terror-stricken. He was obviously desperate to stop the disaster somehow. He promised to finish soon, but couldn't extricate himself from the maze of Biblical verses and Midrashic legends. The din increased. Soon, so it seemed, some impudent lout was bound to leap up and shout, "Enough! It's time for the evening service." The preacher gesticulated and squirmed, as if looking for a word that would calm the crowd, prevent their departure, and make them stay to the end. But there was no such word.

Suddenly the sermon was interrupted. The preacher wiped his perspiration and stared with glazed eyes at the audience. Then his hoarse, despairing voice resounded in the synagogue.

"Good people! I'm a father of eight children. I've been away from home a year and I've left them without a penny. . . . They're probably starving there. Friends . . . merciful Jews . . . have pity on a father of eight children."

A cemetery stillness fell over the bes medresh. A shudder seemed to race through the crowd. No other preacher had ever succeeded in creating such an effect on the audience. Even the rabbi, who by nature hated itinerant preachers, and always fell asleep leaning on his prayer stand during the sermon, even he awoke with a start, sighed deeply, shook his head, and murmured, "Poor man, it's a pity."

And one critic looked gloomily at another and asked, "Did you hear that?"

"Yes," the other answered sadly.

"What a world!" a third man sighed.

The area behind the pulpit where the charity plate lay became congested. Everyone pushed forward to make a contribution for the preacher. Ten-, fifteen-, and forty-kopeck coins flew into the dish like doves.

The next morning two distinguished townsmen went from house to house to collect money. It sufficed for them to say that it was for last night's preacher and a contribution was offered at once. The most generous donation was given by the critic who had said that the preacher "babbled." Looking at the two trustees and the red shawl containing the money, he said with feeling, "It's only right to collect as much as possible. Never mind that he can't preach. But after all, it *is* a pity. He's still a learned man. You know," he concluded with a touch of passion, "I'd be happy to have him here for supper tonight. Why don't you send him over?"

"No," one of the trustees answered, "Yankel Laybes already asked him this morning at services."

Yankel Laybes was the critic who had remarked the night before that the preacher had nothing to say.

A PINCH OF SNUFF

THERE WERE FIVE big synagogues in the little shtetl of Konivke but the small bes medresh was the most impor-tant, because the shtetl's richest citizen, Reb Yakov Sinkess, prayed there. The shtetl people said he was worth two hundred thousand rubles, although in fact he had only one hundred thousand. But even a quarter of that sum would have been enough for the people of Konivke to let him play an influential role. That's why all the prominent household-ers prayed in the small bes medresh; and so did the local religious functionaries — the rabbi, the ritual slaughterer, the tax collector, and a couple of recluses who had served the community for almost ten years.

Also praying among these notables was Grunem, the children's teacher, who was sort of fifth wheel to a wagon here. Downcast since childhood, he had never had the courage to join in the chatting after the Sabbath service, whose focal center was the rich man. Grunem didn't even dare approach and bend an ear to listen. He would stand at a distance and swallow every word coming from the rich man's mouth. No trifle, the stories that Yakov Sinkess had to tell.

First he related how his good friend Count Zapski, whom he visited almost every week, held Jews in high regard. Then he discussed currency rates and the rise and fall of the Russian ruble. (Grunem couldn't even begin to understand. He'd always assumed that a ruble was always a ruble. He wanted to ask the meaning of all this but dared not.) Then the rich man spoke about his recent business trip and his lumber shipment to Koenisberg; how he befriended a Polish priest on his return home, debated matters of faith with him, and emerged victorious. . . . And he told thousands of other tales that only a rich man could know, a man of wealth who conducted his business with supreme confidence and ease.

Grunem would have given half his life for just one word with the rich man. He would have been thrilled. But he never made an attempt. Reb Yakov's affluent demeanor, his imposing height and big paunch somehow kept Grunem away. His full, open face and stern glance frightened the teacher. Grunem was amazed at the boldness of the ritual slaughterer, who at times stood close to the rich man and joined in the conversation. Indeed, one has to have the heart of a slaughterer, Grunem thought, to do what he does . . . but I can't.

Grunem had prayed in the small bes medresh for almost fifteen years without ever speaking to the rich man. He had never had the privilege and never even dreamt of it. When and how could he? Only if Grunem himself were to become wealthy. But how could he become rich? From his young pupils?

Nevertheless, lately Grunem had begun thinking about a chat with the rich man. And not just a chat, but a serious talk.

The mere thought of this conversation sent Grunem's blood rushing to his face. His heart pounded like an armed robber's before a murder. It was no small matter! Grunem had to engage the rich man in a crucial conversation, for he wanted as his pupil the rich man's grandson who would be starting school that summer.

Seeking out a prospective student was nothing new for Grunem. Every term, in a well-rehearsed style, he solicited for some twenty pupils. But what a comparison? With plain householders, it made no difference how one spoke. But with a rich man like Sinkess one had to know what to say. One superfluous word could, God forbid, ruin the whole endeavor.

From Purim to Pesach a great battle raged in Grunem's heart. He wanted to capture a famous general but didn't know how; moreover, he was plain scared.

Pesach was approaching. If Grunem didn't approach Sinkess now, it would be too late and his golden opportunity would be lost forever. What a stroke of luck it would be to have the rich man's grandson as a pupil. First of all the money — he would surely pay fifteen and perhaps even twenty rubles for the term, no doubt about that. The rich man might even give him ten rubles in advance. And what about the prestige! Could one even put a price on that?

Grunem's imagination soared: "Reb Grunem, where does Reb Yakov's grandson study?" "What do you mean, where? Don't you know? Very nice! He studies with *me*. Yes, with me. Can you imagine him sending his grandson to any other teacher? That's all he would need!"

A blissful smile brightened Grunem's gloomy face. But when he gazed at the rich man his entire dream turned to ash and fear seemed to chill his blood. How to approach him? He wished he had legs sturdy enough to stand up under the test. He wished his heart wouldn't hammer so wildly.

The final days of Pesach. Today, at the end of the service, Grunem would have to approach the rich man, although he was sure he would die in the attempt. He collected his thoughts and prepared his little speech:

"Gut yontev, Reb Yakov," Grunem began, then decided that this was too prosaic. That's how he addressed everyone else. He needed a more distinctive greeting. "A very gut yontev, Reb Yakov," would be preferable. But this didn't please him either. He remembered that when Leib the shoemaker got drunk on Simchas Torah he would shout this very phrase to everyone he met. So Grunem concluded that he would indeed say "Gut yontev," but softly and gently. "Gut yontev," he rehearsed. Yes, that would be fine.

And he continued practicing:

"I heard that your grandson, may he live and be well (that would surely please the rich man), is starting school this summer. May it be a happy occasion! I'm Grunem the teacher. Children from the finest homes study with me. I'd like to ask you, Reb Yakov . . ." Or perhaps, he should say, "Our worthy master, Reb Yakov" . . . "to let me have your grandson as a pupil . . . for the sake of neighborliness . . . we pray together. . . ."

But this last reason displeased Grunem. "What sort of neighbor are you to me, you teacher you?" Sinkess might say. "You pray by the rear door and I near the Holy Ark."

Grunem sought another formulation. "For old friendship's sake . . ." Pfui! That's even worse. A new-found friend, the rich man would say and really get angry.

Finally, Grunem settled on this: "I'm a hard worker. In just one term my pupils ride right into Hebrew. Truly right into Hebrew — I have a special method for that."

He reviewed this and found it satisfactory — but the word *ride* smacked too much of a horse and wagon. So he phrased it differently: "In one term I teach them Hebrew according to the rules of grammar." Grunem was finally satisfied with this and hoped that with God's help the rich man would not refuse him.

After prayers Grunem thought it over and decided to approach the rich man resolutely. "It's either or," he braced himself. "Yes, yes. No, no. He certainly won't eat me alive."

The prominent householders were already wishing the rich man a gut yontev. They exchanged only a few words and departed. During the last few days of Passover Reb Yakov had nothing important to relate. His stories had run out during the holiday. The rich man was about to fold his tallis, getting ready to leave.

Grunem slid forward like a shadow. His feet crumbled beneath him. I must take a pinch of snuff from the shamesh, he decided. Maybe that will perk me up.

"Excuse me, shamesh," he asked with a thumping heart. "Give me a bit of snuff."

The shamesh removed the snuff box from his chest pocket. Grunem put two fingers into the box, knocked some snuff out, and contrary to his usual custom, took a very deep sniff. Master of the Universe, he thought, may it be for good health. And he approached the rich man as if drunk.

Now he stood next to him. "Gut yontev, Reb Yakov," he gasped.

The rich man gave Grunem a surprised look. "What is it?"

It's easy to talk to him, Grunem consoled himself. Chin up! Chin up! Just don't get scared, he thought, and gathered courage to continue.

"I . . . have . . . ah . . . ah . . . ah-pshoo!" The snuff made him sneeze suddenly. His eyes filled with tears and he sprayed the rich man's coat and face.

"Pfui! What a vile creature!" Reb Yakov said in a rage and, with a grimace of disgust, waved his hand at Grunem. "Go. Go away. I will have nothing to do with you. Pfui! Sneezing in one's face! What a boor won't do! . . . Shamesh!"

The shamesh rushed over, half dead with fear.

"Who is this . . . this idiot?" the rich man asked, looking angrily at the shamesh.

"A teacher . . . a children's teacher," the frightened shamesh replied.

"What an idiot! Sneezing into one's face! A boor! . . . Pfui!"

"What a disaster!" the humiliated Grunem mumbled to himself as he left the synagogue. "I never take snuff. And of all days, the desire to take a pinch had to come over me today! A new cure-all! If not for this, his grandson would surely have been my pupil. Absolutely! It's the pinch of snuff that did me in."

THE OLD CARPENTER

LEIZER THE CARPENTER was already very old. He walked with a stoop and he obviously needed the cane he held in his right hand. Without it he surely would not have been able to go to the bes medresh. It was the only place he went, for walking was difficult for him, and anyway he had nowhere else to go. His children had left for America and he was as lonely as a stone. His wife had died three years ago, when he was still working. Leizer had worked until he lost his skills — until the day the ax slipped from his hand. It was then that the younger carpenters had told him, "Reb Leizer, it's time to retire. . . ."

He'd been retired for two years. But truth to say, his repose was not complete, for he was burdened by expenses. Somehow he managed with food. A couple of baked potatoes and the head of a herring sufficed him for an entire day. But when he had to pay old Zalmen the two gilden for rent every month it was a calamity. At such times Leizer moved heaven and earth; he did everything he could. Not with his hands, of course, but with his head. He remembered house-holders scattered here and there for whom he had built

houses and who still owed him money. Many of them denied
their debt; others acknowledged his claim but swore they
had no money; and some neither admitted nor denied the
debt but threw him a few gilden anyway.

But of late it had become increasingly difficult for Leizer
to get the two gilden rent money. He already owed old
Zalmen four gilden for two months, and the due date for
the third month was approaching. Zalmen wouldn't have
minded waiting but he could not — he was not the landlord
either. He himself paid rent and it was difficult for him too.
Zalmen was just an old tailor, blind in one eye, and he could
not do much more than patchwork. And how much could
he earn from a patch?

Leizer the carpenter was not angry at Zalmen when on
occasion he demanded the money too harshly, but he
certainly didn't feel good about it. Leizer had never uttered
a lie in his life but now, in his old age, he had fooled old
Zalmen by saying that he'd give him the money today or
tomorrow.

During the past few days Leizer did not leave the bes
medresh after the evening service, but stayed late, looking
into a sacred text in Yiddish translation and waiting for the
clock to strike ten. Leizer was sure that by then old Zalmen
would already be asleep and he could return home.

One day, old Zalmen informed Leizer that he would rent
his room to someone else if he didn't pay him during the
next few days. Leizer became flustered. He muttered,
"Don't be in such a rush. . . . We'll see. . . ." But it was
no more than a murmur. He couldn't say it clearly, for
what was there to see? He quietly took his cane and softly
slipped out of the house.

Leizer was upset by this terrible calamity. As he walked he stared blankly down at the ground and from side to side. As he looked at the houses on his way, his misfortune vanished and he forgot his troubles. The houses became dear to him. Many reminded him of the years gone by when he, tall and vigorous, had worked with gusto. As he passed Yankl the innkeeper's beautiful house he recalled: I worked on this house for ten weeks. Yankl paid honest wages — five gilden a day — and sometimes he would offer me some whiskey after work. And the house was still in good shape. The lumber of long ago was like iron! Leizer stared at another building. But when I built this house I no longer worked for daily wages. Here I was paid a fixed sum. I gave him a wholesale price, and ended up cheating myself. It came to no more than half a ruble or sixty kopecks a day. He couldn't remember exactly. . . .

Now he passed the rich man's house. No little hut, he thought, and was filled with pride. It's already twenty years old and it still looks brand new. It had many rooms, Leizer recalled. He didn't earn too badly working for the rich man — six gilden per day. And he was astonished at the thought of those high wages. Why so much? Because he is the richest man in town, he thought in answer to his own difficult question. Leizer looked at many other houses he had built in the course of his long life. As they returned his greetings he felt a warmth spreading over his old chilled soul, but suddenly his terrible predicament surfaced once more. He recalled the awful thing and his old body trembled. . . .

Despondent, he entered the bes medresh. He recited the afternoon service, and later, the evening service. The clock chimed eight, nine, ten. Old Zalmen must be asleep by now, but Leizer had no intention of returning home yet.

He was reading the ethical text *A Measure of Righteousness*, but his thoughts were elsewhere. The words *What's to be done?* pounded in his old head. They pounded and pounded until they shaped a fortuitous plan. Old Leizer smiled happily, for this was his plan: Henceforth, he would stay in the bes medresh permanently: he would not even return to old Zalmen. He rethought it a few times lest there was a hitch in the idea, but he couldn't find one, and relief overwhelmed him. Of course, of course, he decided resolutely, from now on I'll stay in the bes medresh. A yoke has been removed! No small matter, saving two gilden every month. "Two gilden," he no longer thought, but actually uttered the words out loud. It seemed to him that a great weight had been lifted from his shoulders; his spirits rose.

Nevertheless, a small worry still remained — his debt. He had to pay it, but how? And Leizer sighed again.

The clock in the bes medresh struck twelve and old Leizer dozed at the table. He dreamt that old Zalmen sat at his side, sewing a garment and stabbing him in the eye with the needle with every stitch.

"Reb Zalmen, don't prick me," Leizer pleaded. "I'll pay you the four gilden. Tomorrow I'm starting to work on Yankel the innkeeper's house — he's paying five gilden a day."

But Zalmen turned a deaf ear to this and continued to prick his eye and all his other limbs with the needle. Now Leizer felt that Zalmen was poking him. But the poking was real. The assistant shamesh was standing next to Leizer. He shook him and muttered angrily, "Pardon me, but this is my spot. I have to bed down now."

Leizer began to rub his eyes. Seeing the assistant shamesh instead of old Zalmen he quickly woke up. He remembered his plan of staying in the bes medresh permanently, but before he could say a word the assistant shamesh drily informed him that this wasn't the poorhouse. The trustees had ordered that no one sleep in the bes medresh — it was enough that the yeshiva students slept here.

Finished.

On his way back to old Zalmen, Leizer no longer looked at the houses he had built. The night was very black and Leizer felt even blacker. He purposely slowed his pace to a crawl. He preferred dragging his feet in the dark night to confronting old Zalmen, his debtor. And how would it all end? Old Zalmen would wait another couple of days but no more. Leizer would end up having to stretch out on the street. On the street!

"Oy," he groaned at the thought of it.

Now he remembered his wife's remark of long ago. "Leizer, everyone is building a house. Let's make ourselves a little house too." But his reply was "We can't. No one would pay for my work."

It was a good answer, for she had nothing further to say. Nevertheless, remembering that soon he would have no place to go, his anger at himself grew.

"You old fool!" he reviled himself. "All your life you built houses for other people, but you're going to die on the street."

THE TREE

IT WAS A long street and in this small shtetl it was considered the longest. It had forty little houses and a ruin, in which no one had lived for ten years. All the inhabitants were Jews, except for one goy whom everyone thought of as half-Jewish: he spoke Yiddish, observed many Jewish customs that were beneficial for good health, and lived in a Jewish house with a mezuza on the doorpost. This meant that when poor Jews went begging from door to door, they went to him too. In a year when food was expensive he'd occasionally give them two or three potatoes.

This street had two wells. One with a little rod and the other with a wheel. (The latter was an innovation on the street. At first it upset the older Jews, but later they accepted it.) The street also had an *eruv*, two ditches where the children played in the sand, and two rather deep gutters along each of its sides.

Naturally, the long street, populated with Jews, did not have many trees growing on it. The Jews, all well versed in the sacred texts, knew that long ago in the Land of Israel every Jew had sat under his grapevine and fig tree. They

also knew about the Cedars of Lebanon and other trees
mentioned in the Bible.

But here in the Diaspora they knew very little about trees
and had no inkling how a tree grew. The boys who studied
in cheder passed the word that if apple seeds were planted
a tree would grow. But this was merely a supposition. The
schoolboys had no real faith in it and were too lazy to even
attempt the planting.

Only one solitary tree stood on the long street and
everyone wondered how it got there.

The owner, Chaim Yankl the tailor, also wasn't sure who
had planted the tree and how it grew. Obviously, his father
hadn't planted it, because when Chaim Yankl was a little
boy the tree was as tall and thick as it was now, and Chaim
Yankl's property had no doubt been passed down to him
several generations ago.

On the other hand, perhaps the property had once
belonged to a goy who had planted the tree. Whichever
version was correct, the long street had only one tree, which
belonged to Chaim Yankl the tailor. It stood in front of the
house by the window which faced the street. While he
worked, Chaim Yankl could see his tree, which he loved
more than anything else in the world.

In the fall when the wind blew, the branches shook and
made mournful sounds by the window, as though they
wanted to tell Chaim Yankl a sad story that had no end.
At times like these Chaim Yankl himself grew sad. It seemed
that the needle wanted to leap out of his fingers, so he let
it drop, leaned on the window, and in a reverie hummed
with a half-broken voice, "When Jeremiah walked on ancestral graves . . ."

And then in the little house one could almost hear the soft footfalls of the dead.

In the summer the tree made an even greater impression on Chaim Yankl. Since there was little work, he had time to fantasize about the tree. What's more, during the slack season he rested beneath it. The branches rustled softly and cautiously; sometimes a bird chanced upon a twig and chirped. Chaim Yankl then closed his eyes and meditated upon matters more lofty than shears and pressing iron.

On Sabbath during the summer heat neighbors sometimes came to rest under the tree after their *cholent* lunch.

At such times Chaim Yankl felt very honored. Tuvia, the Talmud teacher, a tall, thin man with sunken cheeks, also came. Yankl greatly admired him and his gentle, pleasant manner of speaking.

"We'll rest a bit under your tree, Reb Chaim Yaakov," said Tuvia softly, stretching out under the tree with a tired smile and not looking at Chaim Yankl as he spoke.

"Oh, with pleasure, Reb Tuvia," Chaim Yankl almost shouted. "With great pleasure. Of course, rest up."

"The trees of the field are human." Tuvia seemed to be overcome by an especially reflective mood as he lay under the tree. "A tree, Reb Chaim Yaakov, is like a man."

And Reb Chaim Yankl looked up and studied the tree's branches and its trunk, as if seeking a similarity between a man and a tree. He did not find any great likeness. Nevertheless, he replied:

"No doubt about it, Reb Tuvia."

"But a tree lives longer," Tuvia immediately contradicted himself, and began to cough deeply and at length.

Every cough echoed in Chaim Yankl's mind like a voice

that said, "Reb Tuvia will soon die. He has tuberculosis and
this tree will outlive us all."

On another Sabbath Zerach Breynes, the rich man of the
street, came to rest under the tree. Zerach had his new suits
made at another tailor's, but Chaim Yankl didn't hold a
grudge. He didn't use his privilege to chase Zerach away
from his tree; on the contrary, he welcomed him with open
arms, to show the rich man that he didn't need his work.

"A nice tree," Reb Zerach praised it, contemplating the
trunk. "If you cut down a tree like this it would provide a
winter's worth of heat. I'm surprised you don't chop it
down, Chaim Yankl."

This suggestion infuriated the tailor. What a pig! he
thought. For him everything is money. But he gave the rich
man a milder response:

"It's forbidden to chop down a tree, Reb Zerach. It's not
permitted and it's a sin even to say it. A tree, says Reb
Tuvia, is like a man."

"The trees of the field are human," Reb Tuvia would
whisper as if in sleep.

"Nonsense. That's only talk." The rich man waved his
hand. "Well, it's time to nap now. Wake me at three so I
can go to have a hot drink."

The tree, however, had one flaw that caused Chaim Yankl
vexation: its fruit.

Had the fruit been good at least, the misfortune wouldn't
have been so great. Chaim Yankl would have spent money
to keep the tree out of the public domain. He would have
fenced it in, or leased it out to Zelig the orchardkeeper, and
thus prevented it from falling into evil hands.

But wild little apples grew on the tree, edible only in late winter, when they were frozen solid after lying in the attic. Even then they tasted so awful one would wish them on one's enemies. But these little apples were good for one thing: to cure carbon monoxide dizziness. During the winter, when everyone got dizzy from the heated pressing irons, Freyde, Chaim Yankl's wife, would save the entire family with these little apples.

But the street urchins didn't care that the apples were wild. After all, they were free. Kids had no patience to wait for them to freeze in the attic, and they didn't fear carbon monoxide fumes. And so in the month of Elul, when the little apples began forming, every day between the afternoon and evening services, the youngsters besieged the tree. They threw sticks and stones at the branches with the most apples, and noisily filled their pockets with the loot.

When he saw the troupe of children by the tree, Chaim Yankl's hands and feet began to tremble and he threw aside his sewing to run out of his house as if his clothes were on fire.

"Bandits!" he shouted. "What do you want from my tree? I'm going to beat you black and blue!"

At first the street urchins were frightened and ran away, shouting and hooting. But when they saw Chaim Yankl returning to his house, they regrouped and beset the tree with renewed energy. This was the beginning of a long and vicious battle. Chaim Yankl began to use weapons. With a stick in hand, he ran like a wild tiger, chasing the children. But they scampered away every time, laughing and shouting, "Hurrah!" and then ran back again.

Sometimes Chaim Yankl lost his patience and pursued the boys for a great distance. This would cause a commotion in the street, and women, children, and bearded Jews rushed out of their houses in a fright.

"What's going on?" they asked one another. "What's happening?"

Soon the cause of the excitement became clear and one person calmed another, saying, "It's nothing. It's nothing. It's only Chaim Yankl the stitcher chasing the boys. Some stitcher! Why is he so stingy with those little apples? All they give you anyway is a stomachache."

These nasty remarks about his little apples added to the tailor's fury and in a rage Chaim Yankl grabbed a youngster and smacked him.

"Oy, oy," the little boy loudly burst into tears. "Why is he hitting me? I didn't even pick any apples."

"Basya! Your little boy is being beaten," a woman shouted, concerned about her neighbor's son.

The mother rushed to her son's defense. "May lightning strike you!" she berated Chaim Yankl. "Why are you hitting my boy? Do you feed him? May worms feed on you! . . . What a scandal! Chaim Yankl has a puny tree with poison apples and the whole street is in a dither."

Everyone on the street began to lash out at Chaim Yankl; some cursed and vilified him, while calm householders only reproved him mildly: "Think about it! You're a Jew with a beard. Aren't you ashamed to be involved in such foolishness? Tree-shmee! It's more befitting a goy, not a Jew. Children pick apples — so let them pick. Are the apples worth anything? Feh! It's disgusting!"

"It's not the apples I care so much about," Chaim Yankl whined. "But they're destroying the tree. They're breaking the branches."

"Branches-shmanches," the calm householders said, re-
suming their moralizing. "Think about it. Aren't you worse
than the children? What kind of business is this? Go home
to your work. Feh! It's disgusting. A Jew with a beard!"

After this reproof Chaim Yankl felt like a child involved
in some mischief. He looked shamefacedly at the preachers,
then at his own beard, gave a foolish smile, and returned home.

Back at home after one such incident, Chaim Yankl stood
by the tree, gazing at pieces of broken twigs scattered on
the ground. At the tip of the tree hung a few broken branches
that looked like corpses. Sighing, Chaim Yankl looked at his
mangled tree and went inside with a heavy heart.

And so from Elul into fall, the street was in a stew — and
the only tree on the street brought lots of life into the
neighborhood.

About ten years passed.

These ten years left their mark on the street. The ruin
was removed by the order of the new police chief who cited
a law about such collapsed houses. Tuvia the Talmud teacher
could not catch his breath during a coughing fit and died.
Zerach the rich man, wanting to increase his wealth, bought
twelve hundred pounds of dried berries on speculation. He
lost all his own money, as well as 25 rubles belonging to
others, and became impoverished.

But the tree on the street still stood. In the autumn,
when the wind blew and the branches rustled sadly, Chaim
Yankl hummed the same melody to the same words from
the Poems of Lament:

"When Jeremiah walked on ancestral graves . . ."

In the summer, the slack season, he still rested under the tree and meditated on matters more lofty than shears and pressing iron. During the month of Elul he still had run-ins with the Talmud Torah boys who besieged the tree. Then the street seethed with excitement: little apples, little boys, tree, Chaim Yankl . . .

Several more years passed.

On Tuvia the teacher's tombstone a few words were already worn away. Zerach the rich man had become totally poverty-stricken. Freyde, Chaim Yankl's wife, died. Chaim Yankl's hair turned white, but the tree still stood. . . .

The tree, however, was not what it used to be.

"I can't understand what's happened to the tree," Chaim Yankl said occasionally, wanting to pour his heart out to someone. "Somehow, it's more bent over and the branches are sparser. It's not what it used to be."

Nobody replied. A foolish tailor. The smell of death, of cemetery leaves, clings to him and he's still obsessed with that tree. He'd be better off saying Psalms and starting to prepare himself for over There.

But Chaim Yankl, gazing with dull eyes and a heavy heart, saw the only tree on the street dying along with him.

"The children have killed it," he cried softly. "The tree is dying."

And Chaim Yankl recalled the words of Tuvia of blessed memory: "The trees of the field are human."

At such moments Chaim Yankl sighed: "He was a scholarly Jew. Too bad he died." Then he leaned against the window, listened to the faint rustling of the few remaining branches, and a wave of deep gloom came over him.

THE LEAP YEAR

"SOON WE'LL TAKE the bread out," Leah said to herself as she opened the oven door and contemplated the six loaves set in two rows.

She looked lovingly at these loaves into which she had obviously poured her entire soul; she sighed deeply and closed the door.

Another half hour, she estimated, looking at the old clock with the broken face that hung between the chest of drawers and the table.

"Mama, you're full of soot," Chashke observed while washing the dishes.

"No matter!" her mother said, waving her hand disparagingly. "It can't compare to the agony of scraping together the ingredients. . . . The pittance your father earns, oh woe unto us!"

Leah recalled what a struggle it had been to bake this bread. Her husband, Shimon, had not earned a kopeck for a month now. The grain trade had become so bad that God's special providence was needed. A peasant bringing to market 250 pounds of oats was besieged by a thousand dealers like locusts, and everyone offered more than it was worth. Such good fortune totally confused the gentile, and he didn't know how steep a price to charge. For the past two weeks Shimon had been making the rounds of the villages to buy grain. Perhaps God would send him something there. . . .

Leah would have continued musing, but she remembered that the wooden shovel had broken when she put the loaves into the oven.

"Now there's no shovel either, praise God," she cried, bemoaning once more the fate of the shovel that she had lamented earlier that morning. "I'll have to go borrow again." With a sigh, she went across the street to her good neighbor Dvoshe.

Whenever Leah went to borrow something, she didn't make her request at once but pretended she had just dropped in for a visit. Only later did she say in passing, "Could you lend me —?"

Now too as she entered Dvoshe's house, she joined the conversation out of politeness.

This time, however, the conversation was so interesting that it distracted her and she forgot why she had come.

They were discussing the leap year.

"Is the second month of Adar far off?" one neighbor asked.

"This Sabbath, if God grants us health, we'll be reciting the prayer for the New Moon for the second month of Adar," Dvoshe answered with scholarly pride.

"And when does the new month begin?" asked another neighbor.

"The new month will begin . . ." Dvoshe wrinkled her brow just like a scholar and then continued proudly: "Let's see now, I'll figure it out in a minute. Since last month the

New Moon came on a Wednesday and Thursday, this one will be on Friday and Saturday. . . ."

"If it weren't for the leap year, it would already be after Purim," the first neighbor remarked.

"Exactly a week after Purim," Dvoshe again displayed her learning.

Leah stood there fascinated. The leap year had caused her many sleepless nights and she expressed her feelings about it with a sigh:

"May the Almighty not punish me for saying this," she began with a singsong melody that the women used while chanting Yiddish prayers in the synagogue. "The leap year lies like a stone on my chest. A year ago at this time, it was already warm. And this year, if it weren't for the leap year, it would probably be warm already. I don't have a bit of wood left."

"What are you talking about? What's the matter with you?" Dvoshe turned to Leah with a sweet smile. "The Almighty with His lovingkindness gives us a month of life as a free gift and you're still not satisfied and sin by complaining."

"No question about it. It is a great gift! Yes, He gives us everything. He gives us our whole life," Leah answered, frightened of revealing her ignorance.

"My goodness!" Dvoshe smiled good-naturedly at Leah's naive response. "That's not what we're talking about. Of course He gives us everything! But nevertheless, God keeps an accounting, as if He has to pay the sinner his due. Every day, every month, every year is reckoned into the accounting and is written into the book. But in the second month of Adar, God doesn't keep accounts. He gives the sinner the second month of Adar as a gift. Like a bonus . . . every three years — an extra month!"

This was an unexpected revelation for Leah. Until now she had thought of the added Adar as a month attached to the long, difficult winter. She hadn't given much thought as to how this month was reckoned up there. Now she had a much clearer idea about the leap year: it was God giving man an extra free month of life!

Now she tried to imagine God as mild and soft hearted . . . standing by a scale with a kindly smile, adding years, months and days, and saying benignly, "Here's an extra month as a bonus. A bonus for Leah, pity on her! Alas, her years are numbered in any case. They're so few. She's already so weak and ill. . . ."

And Leah's face beamed with gratitude out of love for her kind God and she turned to Dvoshe somewhat embarrassed. "I'll tell you the truth. I know nothing at all about this. I'm actually ashamed to admit it."

"What's there to be ashamed about?" Dvoshe smiled good-naturedly. "I read about this in a Yiddish book. My husband says it's also written in the holy Hebrew books."

And the other two neighbors agreed. They had already known this for a long time.

"Can a man's gift, then, be considered a true gift?" Dvoshe began philosophizing: "When He gives, it's really a gift. What can one man, after all, give another? A man has nothing. Everything is His!"

Now the women began talking at length about God's deeds and His lovingkindness toward transgressors. And Leah spoke more than anyone else. The added free month, which would not be included in her reckoning, made her talkative.

She spoke with spirit and verve. All at once it seemed as if her short life had become longer.

"Too bad that the extra month always comes out in the winter." Leah finally managed to find some flaw in God's gift. "God should have made the leap year come during summer. Somehow one is more cheerful during the summer. It's warmer and you don't need any wood."

But Leah caught herself and realized it was a sin to talk like this and immediately changed her tune. "Never mind, let it be winter! One wants another month of life in winter too. . . ."

"One always wants to live," a neighbor sighed.

"Yes, yes," Leah continued. "Living is good and precious, far more precious than livelihood."

Suddenly, she felt a jolt. The word "livelihood" reminded her of the loaves in the oven. She jumped up at once and wringing her hands, cried out in agitation.

"Dvoshinke . . . the bread in the oven . . . quickly, lend me your wood shovel. Oh, woe is me, I chatted too much. It's burnt. . . ."

Rushing into her house with the shovel like a wild beast, Leah opened the oven and quickly threw the baking tins to the ground. She saw the black sheen of the loaves and, not knowing what to do first, wrung her hands in despair. When the first awful moments had passed, and the extent of her misfortune became clear, she began wailing: "Oh, woe is me; oh, woe is me! An entire load of bread ruined! Charcoal! How I scrimped to buy the flour! . . . What should I do now? What can I do now?"

Her small children were frightened and ran to hide in the

corners of the house, but the eldest daughter tried to calm Leah. "Don't be upset. . . . It's not so bad. We'll eat them."

"May the worms eat you, oh dear God!" Leah cursed bitterly. "Couldn't you have come to call me? I got caught up talking, don't ask me about what! Leap year, shmeep year. I couldn't care less."

And contemplating the six shiny black loaves, she began sobbing with a tearful praying chant: "O Master of the Universe! O dear God! You have compassion on all your creatures, why don't you have compassion on me too and take me from this miserable world?"

LOST HIS VOICE

IN THE LARGE bes medresh of Klemenke, the weekday morning service had just ended. Since the shtetl's cantor sang every prayer, even when he prayed by himself, it took him longer to finish. By the time he folded his tallis all the other worshippers were gone. He hummed the melody for the Psalm of the day and concluded the last phrase with a cantorial flourish: "He shall lead us beyond death."

For the last word, he wanted to perform his usual cantorial trick: to ascend one full octave, drop to the normal vocal range, then return quickly to the octave. But he didn't succeed. One of the notes stuck in his throat and it didn't come out right.

This scared the cantor and he looked around in a dither to see if anyone was nearby. When he noticed old Henikh standing next to him, his fright abated somewhat; he knew that Henikh was deaf.

Returning home with his tallis and tefillin under his arm, the failed attempt rang in his ears and saddened him.

"Devil take it!" he said. "This has never happened to me before." He quickly recalled, however, that almost the same thing had occurred two weeks ago, on the Sabbath when they recited the blessing for the New Moon. He was leading the service, accompanied by the choir, and he faltered when he sang the phrase, "He is our God," during the "Hear O Israel" portion of the *Kedusha*. Luckily, no one had noticed. In any case, the bass didn't mention it to him.

The memory of this along with today's quietly sung "beyond death" mingled in his mind and settled like a heavy stone on his heart.

On his way home he wanted to try the octave again, but the street happened to be full of people. The cantor made heroic efforts to restrain himself until he got home. It wasn't like him to rush, but he hurried as if he were fleeing from someone.

He entered his house quietly without saying "good morning," put away his tallis, and rested a while after his quick walk. Then he resumed singing, "He shall lead us beyond death."

"Already? You can't wait? The day's too short?" the cantor's wife complained. "It's grating on my ears as it is."

"What do you mean it's grating?" The cantor gaped in fright. "I'm testing my voice and you say it grates. What do you mean it's grating?"

The cantor's silent, pleading glance seemed to say: Have pity! Don't tell me it grates, because if that's so then I'll be miserable because my life will be done for!

But the cantor's wife was too busy with breakfast to sympathize and try to understand what was happening with her husband.

"Of course it grates, what else?" she shouted even louder. "You're deafening me! If you sing with the choir I suppose

I have to endure it, but why do I have to listen to you solo now?"

The cantor became pale as chalk.

"Gruneh, are you crazy?" he barely managed to say. "What are you talking about?"

"What's wrong with you today?" Gruneh lost her patience. "Stop making a fool of yourself! Go wash and eat!"

The cantor had no desire to eat but thought that he must eat for the sake of his voice. If he didn't, it would be worse, and he went to wash his hands.

He recited the blessing over the bread in a loud cantorial voice, looking at his wife to see if she had noticed anything. But Gruneh said nothing and he felt better.

"It's only my imagination," the cantor consoled himself. It's absolutely nothing! One doesn't lose one's voice so quickly."

But he remembered that he was already forty and exactly the same thing had happened to the cantor Meir Lieder at that age.

This prompted another wave of fear, and holding his head in his hands, he fell into a deep reverie. Suddenly he looked up and shouted, "Gruneh!"

Gruneh came up to him, shouting angrily. "Shush, what's up? Why are you yelling? It doesn't sound like your voice."

"Oh, leave me alone," the cantor pleaded, near tears. "Why are you saying, 'It doesn't sound like your voice'? Whose voice do you think I am using, huh? What do you want from me?"

"You're really crazy today. A nuisance! Well, do you want to eat?" the cantor's wife grumbled.

"Make me a couple of boiled eggs," he said softly.

"A new holiday, huh?" Gruneh was shouting again. "Eggs in the middle of the week! You're going to lead the services on Sabbath? Eggs are so expensive today. Five kopecks apiece."

"Gruneh!" the cantor demanded. "I don't care if it's a ruble an egg, two rubles, five, even a hundred rubles. Do you hear me? Make me two soft-boiled eggs and stop chattering!"

"You really bring in great wages, don't you?" Gruneh mocked him.

"Do you really think it's done for?" The cantor braced himself. "Not so, Gruneh."

He wanted to tell her that he wasn't quite sure — his voice still had some life. It was possible he only imagined it. Maybe he was just deluding himself. But he was afraid to articulate it and Gruneh did not understand what he was muttering. She shrugged and said, "What nonsense!"

She left to boil the eggs. The cantor, meanwhile, began to sing. He paid attention to every note as though he were testing himself. When he couldn't reach a high octave, he shouted in despair, "Gruneh, hurry up and bring the eggs."

Suddenly it seemed to the cantor as if the eggs were his only salvation.

Still grumbling, the cantor's wife served the two boiled eggs.

"Here," she shouted. "We scrimp and save and he's got a yen for eggs!"

The cantor wanted to pour out his heart to her; he didn't want her to think he was interested only in the eggs. He wanted to tell her: Gruneh, I think I'm done for. However, he braced himself and held himself in check.

Perhaps I'm only imagining it, he thought again, and silently began to sip the eggs as though they were a medicine. When he finished he tried a couple of difficult cantorial flourishes. He succeeded and felt better.

No matter, God is good! he thought. I'm not going to lose my voice that quickly. Who cares about Meir Lieder — he was a drunkard. I don't drink except for a bit of wine at a bris.

The cantor's appetite returned and he swallowed one bite after another.

His happiness, however, did not last too long. The earlier failed "death" echoed in his ears and his depression returned.

Throughout his life the cantor had been plagued by the fear of losing his voice. His only constant worry was what would happen when he lost it. In fact, it already had happened once. At seventeen he suddenly lost his tenor, but it hadn't bothered him then. On the contrary, he was pleased because he knew then that his voice was changing. In six months he would become a baritone, a voice he impatiently awaited. When he did become a baritone he realized that if he lost that — that would be it. He would get no other voice. So he tended his voice carefully. When he married and assumed the cantor's position in Klemenke, he wouldn't let a breeze come near his throat — he wore a scarf even during the hottest weather.

Actually, he didn't take care of his voice for the sake of the Klemenke congregants. He was confident that even if he lost his voice entirely, the Klemenke community would not discharge him from his cantorial post. He would always have his wages, and in any case they didn't bring his wages to his house. Every Friday he had to go from house to house and collect the money himself. Klemenke Jews were soft-hearted. They never refused anyone who stretched out his hand. He tended his voice and feared losing it only because he loved singing. The cantor thought very highly of the Klemenke householders: nowhere in the world could one find Jews like these; but in matters of music, they were absolute boors — asses, actually. They had no feeling at all for it. His artistic display of cantorial trills at the highest octave during prayers was done only for the immense pleasure it gave him. He also did it for his eight choristers, of whom he thought very highly. The cantor was very impressed with his singers and when one of them exclaimed, "Oh, cantor, that was beautifully done!" he would be in seventh heaven.

All the choir members had come from various towns and shtetls and the sole focus of all their chats and anecdotes was cantors and vocal music. These tales and legends were the cantor's Zohar. After each story he would be immersed in thought and give out a deep, sweet sigh.

"No small matter, vocal singing! The feeling for it is no trifle."

Now that the cantor was afraid of losing his voice, he constantly thought that his choristers had changed for the worse. They laughed at him behind his back, no doubt, and he was careful not to take any high notes lest they find out. And he suffered even more on account of this.

What would the cantors of the neighboring towns say? This thought was an even greater torment. He knew he had a reputation among the cantors in the region. They thought very highly of him and spoke often about his voice. He imagined a group of cantors standing talking quietly about him, sadly shaking their heads, feeling pity. "Tsk, tsk, alas, have you heard that the Klemenke cantor . . ."

Such a thought would drive him completely out of his mind.

Perhaps I'm only imagining it, he told himself. In such awful moments he would begin to console himself and immediately begin to sing, trying to reach the highest notes. But fear made him lose his sense of hearing and he could not tell if his voice was functioning as usual.

Within two weeks his face became pale and drawn, his eyes sunken. He felt his strength ebbing.

"What's wrong with you, cantor?" one of the choir singers asked him.

"What? What's wrong with me?" The cantor panicked, assuming that they had discovered his terrible secret. "What's wrong with me, you say? Do you notice something, eh?"

"No. I don't know. That's why I'm asking you. Why are you so upset?"

"Upset, you say? Upset? No more than upset, huh? No more than that?"

The singers assumed that the cantor must be thinking about a magnificent new piece for the holidays.

Another month passed by and his fear did not subside. The cantor was sick and tired of living like this.

If he could be certain that he had lost his voice, perhaps he might have calmed down. Done for! A man can't live forever (losing his voice and dying was all the same for him). But the doubts, the high hopes alternating with deep despair — all of this embittered the cantor's life.

One Thursday, prior to the Sabbath when the blessing for the New Moon is recited, the cantor decided to find out the truth — he couldn't stand it any longer.

It was evening. His wife had gone to the butcher for meat and the choristers had left. The only one who remained in the house was the cantor and the oldest singer, Yosl the bass.

The cantor tried to speak but couldn't. It was difficult for him to express his thoughts. Finally, he burst out, "Yosl!"

"What is it, cantor?"

"Tell me, are you an honest man?"

Yosl stared at the cantor and asked, "How come you're asking me this today?"

"Dear brother Yosl." The cantor almost burst into tears. "Brother, Yosl . . ."

He could not utter another word.

"Cantor, what's the matter with you?"

"Brother Yosl! Be an honest man and tell me the truth. The truth!"

"I don't understand what's the matter with you."

"Tell me the truth. Do you notice any change in me?"

"Yes, a big one," Yosl answered, noticing how pale and drawn the cantor had become. "A very big change."

"Now I see you're an honest man. You're telling me the truth right to my face. How long have you noticed this?"

"Probably about a month," Yosl answered.

"Yes, brother, a month. A month. But I've felt . . ."

The cantor wiped the perspiration from his forehead and continued: "And what do you think, Yosl? Do you think I've lost it forever?"

"Lost what?" Yosl asked, realizing that it was something entirely different.

"You still don't know? What can I lose, money? I don't have any money. Naturally, I'm referring to my voice."

This Yosl had already understood. He was too much of a singer not to understand it. With a commiserating look, he gazed at the cantor and asked, "Are you sure?"

"What, sure?" The cantor cheered up. "Perhaps I'm not sure. On the contrary, on the contrary, I wish it were all a mistake."

Yosl looked at the cantor, and like a doctor examining his patient, he told him, "Sing *do*."

The cantor obeyed and, like a pupil, sang *do*.

"Sing it out, stretch it out, four quarters more," Yosl ordered, listening carefully.

The cantor continued the note.

"Now, if you don't mind, sing *re*."

The cantor stretched out the *re-re-re*. Yosl paused, thought deeply, and said sadly, "It's not what it used to be. Lost."

"Permanently?" The cantor gaped at him in fright. "Really?"

"Of course! You're no youngster. Do you expect to get another voice again? At your age it's finished."

The cantor wrung his hands, ran to the table, and placing his head in his hands, began crying like a baby.

The next morning the entire shtetl knew about the misfortune. The cantor had lost his voice.

"Big deal!" Yaakov the innkeeper, a worthy householder, belittled the cantor's tragedy. "So on the Sabbath when they bless the New Moon he won't keep them in their seats so long with his chirping. I wouldn't give you a rotten onion for his entire voice."

REISELE

WHEN EIGHT-YEAR-OLD Reisele woke up in the morning, she rubbed her sleepy eyes and gazed at all four corners of the room looking for something.

She was looking for her mother, Chiyeneh, but she had already left for the marketplace with her basket of apples.

Reisele sighed. "Gone so quickly?"

She languidly put on her old, torn little dress, washed, found a rag that resembled a towel, and dried herself. Now her head cleared a little, and she recalled that today was Tuesday and that all night long her mother had been gasping for breath. She had brought her cold water and a piece of sugar, but to no avail. Chiyeneh had stared at her so strangely. "Reisele," she had said, "do you feel sorry for me?" Reisele had not answered but burst into tears and ran to a corner to cry. More than that she did not remember. She only knew that she had dreamt all night long.

She must be feeling better, Reisele consoled herself. Otherwise she would not have gone to the marketplace.

On the table Reisele found breakfast prepared for her —a piece of bread and some milk in a broken glass.

When she finished eating, she felt gloomy. She prayed to God for darkness to fall so her mother would return. During the summer she could not restrain herself and would run to the market to see how her mother was faring. Even though her mother always complained that there was no business, Reisele enjoyed being with her. When a customer approached her mother's basket of apples and bought something, she cried out in delight, "Mamele, you're making a sale!"

But for the most part Chiyeneh would answer sadly, "Ah, woe to such sales, my child. It's only the third kopeck for the entire day.

During the winter Reisele didn't even have this small pleasure. She had never owned a pair of shoes, and it was too cold to run to the market barefoot. Mother had warned that she might catch cold and die, God forbid. And dying, Reisele knew, was a very bad thing. She did not remember when her father had died, but she knew that he was in a deep grave in the cemetery behind the town and could never return from there, not even during the summer. Never! That's why she was very careful. So during the winter she sat home all day long, waiting for dark, when her mother would return.

She kept going to the window. "It's dark already," she said. "Soon. Soon she'll come home."

Nevertheless, she had to wait a long time. Darkness fell over the little house with its frosted windows, but outside there was still light. Time stretched unbearably for Reisele.

"It's dark already." She sighed impatiently. "Why doesn't Mama come?"

The darkness thickened in the little house. By now Reisele could only see a part of the stove, which her mother had recently whitewashed. When she heard a knock at the door, her little heart almost jumped out of her chest with joy.

"Mama's coming!" she sang out. "Mama's coming!" No one else ever came, she knew. And indeed her mother had come in almost frozen. She set the basket by the door and called, "Where are you, Reisele?"

"Here I am, Mama. Here, next to the bed. Make light." Chiyeneh struck a match and lit the lamp. It was only a dim light that glowed in the little house, but it was enough for Reisele — all she needed was a glimpse of her mother. She saw her quite clearly standing in front of the smoky lamp and it made her happy.

"Mama, are you going to cook supper?"

"Of course," she replied. "You're probably hungry."

"No, I don't want to eat, but you probably do."

"I don't want to eat, either. I bought half a pound of bread at the market and ate it with a rotten apple. It was delicious."

Mama lit a fire. When the flames took hold, she set a pot of water to boil and sat down with Reisele. Looking at the fire and at her mother, Reisele felt so good and so warm.

The pot of water began to boil merrily. Chiyeneh cooked some barley and half an hour later both were eating supper.

At the second bite, Mama began coughing. Reisele stopped eating and waited for her mother's spell to pass. Chiyeneh wanted to tell Reisele, Eat, don't wait! But the cough choked her and she couldn't utter a word.

"Mamele, enough coughing," little Reisele pleaded with tear-filled eyes.

"Let me indulge in a bit of coughing," her mother said when her fit had ended, stroking Reisele's hair.

But instead of an answer, Reisele threw her arms around her and burst into tears.

Reisele had turned twelve.

It was summer. The powerful rays of the sun penetrated even through the small dust-covered windows and shone on Reisele's small face. Reisele, who had been sad all morning long, was revived by the sweet light, which made her want to go out to the street. . . . But what would she do there? She had no one to play with. All the girls her age wore little dresses and Reisele didn't even own shoes. Everyone was ashamed of her. She had only one friend —her mother. Mama was so kind, so good. Her sweet mother acquiesced to her every wish. She even obeyed when Reisele asked her to stop coughing when she came home from the market. During the night, however, Reisele's requests were of no avail. This past night her mother had coughed so much. . . . Reisele had brought her water two times, but it didn't help. . . . Why was Mama coughing so much? She said it was a disorder, but one could live out one's years with it. *Her* mother, Mama said — that is, Grandmother — had also had this problem and she too had lived out her years. . . . "Oh God, let Mama live!" Reisele's little heart began to cry. She imagined her mother's pale face and longed to be close to her. Their little house became even more cramped. The thought, "I must go to the market," flashed through Reisele's little head. To Mama . . .

Barefoot and in her old torn dress, she quickly ran to her mother.

"Why did you come, Reisele?" Chiyeneh asked kindly.

"Just like that, Mama. I feel sad," Reisele answered shyly.

"Well, no harm done," her mother consoled her. "Stay here, there's no business anyway."

A market peddler who sat opposite her left her little stool and approached both of them. She usually squabbled with Reisele's mother over every kopeck's worth of business but became friendly when neither of them had sales.

She contemplated Reisele with penetrating glances and called out, "You know, Chiyeneh, your Reisele is growing, may the evil eye spare her."

"May her good fortune grow the same way," Chiyeneh sighed, looking with brimming eyes at her small, thin child.

"What do you mean?" the other woman continued. "One year will pass and then another, and soon she'll be a young lady and will have to have a bridegroom. The years fly by. How long has it been since I myself was a youngster? It seems like only yesterday . . . and quite a pretty girl too," the peddler concluded, looking at Reisele's curly locks on her broad forehead and at her pale face and deep black eyes.

Reisele couldn't bear the peddler's gaze. Two red spots appeared on her pale face and she became even prettier.

"A beautiful girl indeed!" The peddler continued complimenting her.

"May her fortune be as beautiful as she!" Chiyeneh sighed. "God Almighty, may her father be a good interceder for her in heaven!"

"Of course," the peddler answered. "Who then if not he? Still, Chiyeneh, you should start thinking what to do with her. It's not practical the way it is."

"Well, what should I do," the mother sighed, "make her stand with a basket of apples? I myself don't do any business."

"Why a basket of apples?" the peddler cut her off, as though afraid of another competitor. "Why don't you find a job for her in someone's house? Nowadays that's nothing to be ashamed of." Chiyeneh and Reisele exchanged glances. Both paled. They looked sternly at the peddler as though they were chiding her: You bandit! You want to separate us?

Reisele did not leave her mother's side. She waited until dark and both returned home together. They didn't exchange a word during the walk home, as if both had suddenly become mute. Occasionally, Reisele would take hold of her mother's dress, as though frightened of something.

It was already dark when they came home. Reisele started a fire. The two big tears running down her mother's drawn, sallow face scared her.

"Mamele, you're crying!" she called out in alarm, huddling next to her.

"Did you expect me to laugh? Isn't the peddler right? Oh woe is me! You're already a girl of twelve and you don't even have a pair of shoes or a blouse to cover yourself. I'm sick and God only knows how I'll manage to stay at the market. . . . What will become of us?"

"So what should I do?" Reisele asked. "If I could earn money, I'd have a dress and shoes made and I'd also order a pretty dress for you for the holidays.

Chiyeneh, silent for a while, gazed wide-eyed at her little daughter. Then she asked softly, "Reisele, do you want to earn money?"

"Oh, yes." Reisele looked up. "If only I knew how! I'd really like to be a seamstress. Sara's daughter Leah who lives opposite us is a seamstress. And she earns so much money. Every Sabbath I see her walking in such a beautiful dress. And even during the week she wears a little cap. But I wouldn't wear a little cap: I'd rather buy you a new wig. Yours is already all torn."

"No, my child," her mother interrupted. "Being a seamstress is not for you. It would take three years before you started earning money and you still wouldn't be able to buy a dress. When you get apprenticed to someone, you have to give the shop owner ten rubles for teaching you the trade."

"Well, then, how does one earn money?" Reisele asked sadly.

"You heard what the market peddler said."

Reisele's pale face became even paler. Fear floated in her deep little eyes. "And leave you alone, Mama? At night you wouldn't even have anyone to give you some cold water."

Chiyeneh did not reply, but two more tears ran down her somber eyes onto Reisele's little face.

"Come, Mama, don't cry," Reisele begged. "You'll find me a job at a nice lady's house and she'll let me come home every night to sleep with you."

"No, my child, there are no nice housemistresses. If they pay wages, they want to make use of you day and night."

"But don't they have any pity?" Reisele asked, apprehensive.

Her mother did not respond. A definite no would frighten her one and only beloved child, who would surely fall into the hands of such a woman. But her tongue wouldn't let her utter yes either. All the housemistresses she'd known were mean-spirited. And so Chiyeneh remained silent.

Eight days later Reisele arrived at the home of Madame Glotzman.

"Just do your work well," were Madame Glotzman's first words. "Everyone likes someone who works efficiently and well. And I want you to do everything you're told to do.

You must obey everyone, even the cook, and then things will go well for you here."

Reisele gaped at the big, fat Madame. She could not understand how things would go well for her here, if this big fat Madame Glotzman fed her and told her, "Go to sleep," and if this fat Madame Glotzman ordered her to perform a task and never said, "My child," "My daughter," or even "Reisele," but always called her just "you."

No, you're a big liar; you're wicked! Reisele thought the first night as she lay on the little bed in the kitchen. Things can't go well for me here. Things are good *there*, in the little house beside my sick mother. This place is a prison for me. At night Mama will cough there, and I'll have to work here. And why does this big fat mistress need me? Does she cough like my mother? She's so healthy. And if she were to cough even once, she would have so many people here to bring her wine, while there my mother lies all alone and coughs and coughs, calling, "Reisele, Reisele, some water, Reisele, some water . . ." Reisele quickly clambered out of bed, went to the window, and looked for the little house where her mother lay alone.

"Mama, Mama, dear Mama," she called and, unable to contain herself, began weeping, burrowing her head into the pillow.

Her weeping, however, woke no one. Everyone slept soundly.

TEN POUNDS LESS

ON THE MORNING after Purim, Beyla immediately began to worry about matza.

"It's time to start thinking about matza," she said, turning to her husband Zerach with an anxious face.

Zerach stroked his beard thoughtfully, then raised his hand and said proudly, "Yes, there will be matza! With God's help we won't eat *chometz*."

Her husband's assertive tone and the bit of faith that poverty had not totally stolen from Beyla had their effect; she did not mention matza again for an entire week.

But when the week ended and matza baking had already begun in the shtetl and women were pestering one another about Passover flour — which? where? how much? — Beyla raised the subject again.

"Zerach, Passover is only three weeks away! What are we going to do about matza?"

This time Zerach stroked his beard feebly. Instead of raising his hand, he hummed a little melody from a liturgical hymn sung on the Sabbath before Purim. Finally, he answered with exaggerated confidence: "Have you ever eaten *chometz* on Passover?"

"Let's say you're right," Beyla answered, "but we have to see about getting some money. After all, Passover flour is not regular flour and no one will lend us money and today the price of flour is sky high. People say that all the mills have been flooded. No trifle, those floods. It was snowing all winter long."

"Don't worry. You'll have enough for flour," Zerach said, to calm her, "just like every year."

In truth, however, deep down Zerach was even more frightened than Beyla. He knew more about the floods than she did. Indeed, the mills had been inundated and the price of Passover flour could rise to two rubles for a forty-pound bag.

And so Zerach pulled out all the stops to think of a way to get money for matza. He wouldn't take any from the Matza Fund, may God protect him from such a disgrace. Although Zerach was a poor man and had been unemployed for several years, he was nevertheless a householder; he had his own little house in the shtetl and a seat in the bes medresh. And he himself, according to his status, had been assessed for a half-ruble donation to the Matza Fund. And he would give it, even if it cost him his life, even if his beard turned white and more wrinkles lined his large forehead, and even if he had to give the moneylender an IOU.

Several days later, after his last conversation with Beyla, Zerach came home with ten rubles for Passover.

"Well, thank God, now we'll have enough for the holiday," he announced happily as he showed Beyla the money. But then, remembering how he got it and how he would have to pay it back, he sighed. "O dear Father in heaven, it's a bitter world!"

"How much should we bake this year?" Beyla interrupted his sighs.

"How much did you bake last year?"

"Last year we baked ninety pounds of flour."

"Well, then, why don't you bake the same amount this year? Why are you asking?"

"But perhaps eighty pounds would be enough," Beyla suggested.

"I don't care!" Zerach shouted.

"But what if it's not enough?"

"Then bake ninety pounds."

"But I want to save money. We won't have enough to prepare for Passover. Ten rubles is like a drop in the ocean."

And Beyla began reckoning. She would definitely need thirty eggs. Without them the matza balls fall apart and have no taste. Then she would have to buy at least two pounds of chicken fat, a couple of ropes of onions, three small ladles, spoons and glasses. Then Beyla suddenly recalled that she would have to kosher the copper pans.

"Don't forget the wine," Zerach said with a bitter smile.

"Yes, wine," Beyla realized. "There won't be enough money."

"And do you still have potatoes?" Zerach remembered another item.

"Praise God, there are no potatoes either. We'll just have to bake eighty pounds of flour," she finally resolved. Ten pounds of flour cost half a ruble, she thought, and baking it would cost another quarter of a ruble. Those seventy-five kopecks could come in very handy. . . .

"So let it be eighty pounds." Zerach relented.

"Eighty pounds is enough," Beyla cried out, then immediately declared, "But what if we run out of matzas, God forbid?" And a shiver ran through her heart.

In the end, Beyla baked only eighty pounds of flour.

Earlier, when buying the flour, a flutter of anxiety had passed through her. Who knows what kind of mistake she was making? After all, a household of eight people, and all of them good eaters, may the evil eye spare them. Even the smallest one, Leybele, ate like an adult, constantly asking, "Mama, what to eat?" They might run short.

Beyla imagined that for the last two days of the holiday all the matza was gone. The street would be abuzz: At Beyla's house there's no matza left . . . and compassionate women would go from house to house collecting matza for Beyla.

"Add ten pounds to the eighty," Beyla suddenly shouted to the shopkeeper who was already pouring the flour into a soft sack with a shovel.

"Ten more it is," the shopkeeper said impassively, just to show that the extra ten pounds made no difference to him.

But Beyla immediately regretted her decision; in her head another reckoning was taking place: Ten pounds equals seventy-five kopecks, which could come in handy for wine and potatoes. Already there was hardly anything left of the ten rubles. They had simply melted away.

"Stop! Just weigh out eighty pounds even," she said with a start.

"You don't know what you want," the shopkeeper grumbled. "You're driving me crazy."

"I want to save some money," Beyla said with a dejected smile and her pale cheeks reddened in embarrassment.

"Eighty pounds," the shopkeeper declared, looking very intently at the scales.

It seemed to Beyla that the scales were not quite even.

"I think just a bit is missing."

"It's right on the button. Not a drop is missing," the shopkeeper said confidently and added another bit of flour.

Beyla was delighted with the extra flour. Her face began to shine and she suddenly felt an urge to confide in the shopkeeper.

"What do you think, Reb Chaim? Won't eighty pounds be too little? There are eight people in our family."

"How can you say too little or too much?" Reb Chaim began to philosophize. "It depends on the dishes you prepare. In our house we use only forty pounds of matza for the nine of us, but that's because my Sarah makes a potato pudding every day."

"I make a potato stew every day," Beyla confided.

"That's also good," the shopkeeper replied. "A potato stew also saves matza. A potato pudding, however, is even more economical, but it likes a lot of chicken fat."

Beyla realized that she couldn't afford the same items as the rich shopkeeper. He probably ordered twenty pounds of meat for the holidays, not to mention fish! For him the matza was insignificant, even secondary. But for Beyla matza was the most important thing, and again a wave of fear came over her.

There won't be enough matza. . . .

While they were baking Beyla's matzas, a measure of dough was declared unfit for Passover use by the bakery's *mashgiach.* In the middle of the baking, Beyla wanted to run out and buy ten more pounds of flour, but the owner calmed her. Beyla would have enough flour, she said, and out of the dough declared unfit for Passover matzas she could always make farfel for use before the holiday.

Beyla, distraught, let herself be persuaded.

But when her matzas were done and the porter put them into two baskets, the amount seemed so small that Beyla's fear increased. This year, her heart wept silently, we won't have any matza for the last two days of Passover.

The matza was brought home. The smaller children surrounded the baskets and stared at them with ravenous little eyes.

"Matza, matza," they sang. "I want a piece of matza."

"You bandits!" the worried Beyla said with a start. "We're going to run short. It's not like last year. This year I baked only eighty pounds."

"Give them a little bit," Zerach interceded for them.

"No, you're not allowed to eat it before Passover. God willing, we'll eat it during the holiday."

The children left disappointed. Even Beyla felt a twinge in her heart. She was about to call them back and give them some matza, but she stopped herself. This year we'll have to eat the matza sparingly, she decided against her will. I won't urge them to have more.

"How much matza did you bake this year, Beyla?" one of her neighbors asked on the morning before the Seder, just after the *chometz* was burned.

"Eighty pounds," Beyla answered sadly.

"Won't it be too little?" the neighbor said matter-of-factly.

Beyla's heart sank and she barely managed to respond, "It will be enough."

"I have a smaller household," the neighbor continued, "and, thank God, I baked ninety-five pounds. I'd rather have it left over than run short. This year, they say, the flour didn't give much yield."

"Children!" Beyla commanded as she entered her house after talking with the neighbor, "Don't stuff yourselves with matza during the holiday, you hear! If we're not careful, we'll be left without matza."

The children exchanged frightened glances.

"What should we eat then, bread?" the older girl asked ironically.

Beyla, exasperated and enraged, regretted everything she'd done and lashed out at the children: "Eat plagues! Eat worms! Just don't eat matzas!"

"Look, I beg you, please don't spoil the holiday," Zerach pleaded. "Everything is such a struggle. Let's at least enjoy it. Why don't you prepare the wine flask? It's up there on the shelf."

"So you've got lots of money for wine, have you?" Beyla asked.

"Seventy-five kopecks," Zerach answered shamefacedly.

"Twenty-five kopecks should be enough for wine and with the other fifty kopecks we'll have to buy potatoes, understand? Because we're not going to have enough matza. This year the flour didn't give much yield."

When Beyla had bought 125 pounds of potatoes from a gentile woman on the street she became a little calmer.

Throughout the holiday she let the children eat as much matza as they wanted, but up to the last two days of the holiday she herself — except for reciting the blessing over the matza — did not even taste a piece of it. Every morning, she would bake potatoes and dip them into lots of salt, and instead of eating during Passover, all she did was drink lots of water.

A WOMAN'S FEAR

CHIYENE FELL ASLEEP with a good idea: Tomorrow, God willing, she'd cook chickpeas and potatoes for lunch. It would be something new and her husband, Leybe, would be pleased.

As the pale morning dawned into the small house, Chiyene was already awake. She poured some water from a pitcher over her fingers, said the blessing, remembered the "good idea" that had come to her just before she'd fallen asleep, and began preparing the few chickpeas that awaited her in the kitchen.

The children and Leybe were still fast asleep. The house was quiet. Only the rooster in the coop, which Chiyene was saving for Yom Kippur, disturbed the silence every five minutes with his crowing.

Chiyene poured the chickpeas from the paper wrapping onto a small tablecloth that covered half the table; she raked a small heap from the large one and began examining each chickpea. The wormy ones she threw into a glass and the clean ones into a plate. She inspected each little pile three times lest, God forbid, any wormy chickpeas remain and lest she lose her share in the World to Come — for eating a wormy chickpea was ten times more traif than pork. Thus her mother had taught her when she was young.

After sorting out half the peas, she began to see spots before her eyes. A haze came over the chickpeas and she found it difficult to check them. She touched every wormy pea with her fingers more than she examined it with her eyes.

Everything seems to be darker, she thought, and began to get frightened. She wasn't sure anymore if every chickpea she threw into the plate was clean.

At first the thought of being responsible for such a sin distressed her. Her poor eyesight might cause her to throw wormy chickpeas into the plate instead of clean ones. But soon a much greater fear enveloped her: she was only thirty-eight and already her vision was dimming.

She recalled that lately when she read her Yiddish Bible on Sabbath afternoon and cried at the sad stories, a film seemed to cover the words like a veil and reading became a difficult and painful chore.

"I've cried my eyes out prematurely. At thirty-eight," she sighed, sitting with her head bent over the heap of chickpeas.

Chiyene reminded herself that she had spent her entire life in tears. When she was a youngster she cried over every pair of shoes, every dress that her poor father ordered for her. When she was engaged, she cried over every instance of stubbornness on the part of her fiancé, who continually threatened to break off the match and send back the engagement contract if this or that condition was not met. She cried as she stood under the wedding canopy, reminding herself whom she was marrying. After the wedding she cried when Leybe shouted at her for the first time, and who could even count the tears she had shed during pregnancy, at childbirth, over sick children's cradles . . . and by the small graves which she would visit every Tisha B'Av.

"A lot of tears," she concluded and sighed again.

But that wasn't all, she soon recalled. She had shed many more tears reading the Yiddish Bible — over the Binding of Isaac, the selling of Joseph, Pharaoh's decree to throw all male Israelite babies into the Nile, the destruction of the Holy Temple. Her entire Bible had become yellow with tears.

But most yellow were the pages of the weekly Torah portion *Vayetze*, which deals with Rachel and Leah and how our forefather Jacob preferred Rachel to Leah. When she was growing up, Leah had weak eyes from crying. She was afraid that the evil Esau would become her husband, which she had foreseen by power of the divine spirit.

I had a feeling this would happen, Chiyene thought, remembering the tears she had shed over Leah's ill fortune when she was young.

She was also sure that from now on, Leybe would hate her even more. If the saintly Jacob had disliked Leah for her weak eyes, then surely Leybe would despise her too. He would shout at her even louder, and make fun of her more often. "Hey, beauty!" he would say. And who knows, perhaps he'd even call her "No eyes!"

The last thought tormented her. She tried to drive it away and strained her eyes to the utmost to sort out the clean chickpeas.

"It's still rather dark," she consoled herself. "That's why I don't see so well."

But when she looked out the window and saw that it was quite light outside, her consolation vanished.

About an hour later everyone at home had risen. Her sixteen-year-old daughter, Yentl, dressed quickly and began to help her mother, who had already heated the oven.

"Mama, what should I do?" Yentl asked.

Chiyene quickly looked at all four corners of the room, as if she were about to reveal a secret. When she was sure that Leybe was gone, she answered softly and weakly, as though she'd just gotten up from a sick bed. "Look over the chickpeas, my darling."

"You still haven't sorted them out, Mama?"

"Yes, I have but — who can tell? — suppose I left a few wormy ones in there? My eyes aren't as good any more, my child. We might end up eating something traif, God forbid. A wormy chickpea is as traif as pork."

Yentl sat at the table to inspect the chickpeas again and every once in a while she joyfully announced, "Here's a wormy one . . . and here's another. . . . Oh my, how many wormy chickpeas you let slip through! What were you thinking of?"

This question cut through Chiyene's heart like a blunt knife.

"I can't see anymore," she answered bitterly.

Yentl's eyes opened wide with fright; she didn't know what to say.

"Your father will divorce me," Chiyene added with a forced smile.

Yentl gave an anguished grimace.

"Oh, Mama, don't say that."

"What's the matter, silly girl, isn't it so? Your father is still a young man and I'm already an old woman. I can't see anymore."

"Dear God! That's enough, Mama!" Yentl shouted, pretending to be angry, but scarcely able to restrain her tears. From week to week, Chiyene's eyesight dimmed and her fright grew. It seemed to her that Leybe became colder every day. He scarcely looked at her, and as soon as he finished eating in the morning he left for the marketplace.

Besides her fear of her husband, Chiyene also suffered on shabbes in shul, especially while reading the techines, the Yiddish women's prayers. The techina recited when the Torah was taken from the Holy Ark she knew by heart. But on the Sabbath when the Blessing for the New Moon was said, she looked enviously at the other women, who sat proudly holding their prayerbooks, reading with ease and crying. She would bring the prayerbook closer to her eyes and make an effort not to cry (although, alas, what good was a techina without tears — like a wedding without musicians?). But this was of little help. The letters seemed to fuse on the page. She could barely make out a word, except for the large-type first words of each prayer that began with "Master of the Universe . . ." The bigger words were in Hebrew, however, hence holier, and the merit derived from them would perhaps be even greater in the World to Come. Still, they were somewhat unfamiliar. She didn't understand them. But her Yiddish words, which were printed in small, pearl-like letters and spoke to her heart and were so precious and close to her — these little letters played tricks on Chiyene, as if on spite. They wanted to tease her. As soon as she began to pray, they started jumping and hiding beneath a black veil.

"What kind of sin have I committed, God Almighty?" Chiyene wept softly as she sat in shul holding the techina book. "Why have you punished me at such a young age, sweet Father?" Thus on the Sabbath, she was deprived of her only joy and consolation. Fearing that Leybe might become suspicious about her eyes if she did not read, she spent the same amount of time with the Bible as she usually did. Instead of concurrently reading and crying, as had been her habit, now she cried only at her own misfortune. And Leybe, upon waking up from his post-cholent nap, would shout, "What's my little saint all excited about?"

An echo of "Old woman!" rang in Chiyene's ears, and she would quiet down.

Once, in shul on a Sabbath, she confided her complaint to the rebbetzin. The rabbi's wife was a woman with a wrinkled face who looked much older than she was. Her sad, kindly black eyes gazed piously from behind her glasses, which she wore while reading the techines, as if they were expressing a yearning for other worlds.

"What should I do, rebbetzin?" Chiyene asked her during the Torah reading. "I can't see the letters anymore."

"So buy a pair of glasses, my child," the rebbetzin said to console her.

Chiyene shivered.

"It's only fifteen kopecks and then you'll be able to read," the rebbetzin continued, noticing Chiyene's embarrassment.

"I'm only thirty-eight, rebbetzin!" Chiyene said weakly. "I'm ashamed."

"I believe you, my child. I too was ashamed once. . . . In fact, I'm still ashamed, and I've been wearing glasses for two years now. Of course, you're ashamed at first. But what's to be done? Come, for the fun of it, try mine. I think they'll be good for you."

The rebbetzin took the glasses off her thin nose and with a friendly smile put them on Chiyene's.

The colors changed on Chiyene's face. She turned first red and then white, like a young girl trying on a man's hat.

"Now see if you can read a bit from my techina."

The rebbetzin gave her the techina and Chiyene looked into it with a beating heart.

"Well?" the rebbetzin asked like a doctor. "Can you see?"

"What a question!" Chiyene replied happily. "All of a sudden everything is bright and clear, just like a month after my wedding."

"Master of the Universe," she read, "sense Thou the longing of my heart to do good and cause me to do Thy will and hearken unto my prayer and cause Thy Divine Presence to rest upon us so that the spirit of wisdom and understanding encompass us, and may the verse be fulfilled that declares, 'And the spirit of the Lord and the spirit of wisdom shall rest upon him. . . .' "

"This prayer," the rebbetzin interrupted, "you're familiar with, since you say it every Sabbath. So this one is no proof that these glasses are good for you. Try reading from this techina, it's brand new. You've never seen this one before."

The rebbetzin adjusted the glasses on Chiyene's nose and remarked that they should be worn higher. Chiyene gave a sickly smile and let herself be tested on the brand new techina.

"Master of the Universe! Thou art the Creator of mankind and Thou hast created him with a body and a soul. The body is comprised of *ofor min ho-adomo* . . ."

"Dust of the earth," the rebbetzin interrupted, translating the Hebrew phrase quickly and eagerly, like a thirsty man seizing the pitcher from another man's hand while he's still drinking.

"Dust of the earth," Chiyene continued, falling more and more into the sad singsong of the techina chant. "And the soul emanates from Thy holy Throne of Glory, and when man dies, body and soul separate, and each goes to its own place. The body is put into the grave . . ."

"Of course it's buried," the rebbetzin interjected. "The sinful body isn't kept. . . ."

"The body is put into the grave and it rots and returns to the earth . . ."

"Well, enough," the rebbetzin interrupted. "You see how well you read with these glasses?"

"And how! As if I were born again!" Chiyene was delighted. "Like a month after my wedding."

"So, God willing, after Sabbath, you'll buy yourself a pair of glasses and everything will be bright again."

Chiyene fell into a sad reverie. Wearing the glasses made her look old and ugly, she thought. She imagined herself with the glasses as she sat reading the Yiddish Bible on Sabbath afternoon. Leybe would wake up from his nap, approach the table, grimace angrily as he looked at her, and mutter, "Old crone!"

She wouldn't be able to control herself. "If you don't like it," she would say, "you can divorce me if you wish."

"Gladly, even tomorrow," her husband would snap back happily.

And Leybe would keep his promise. She was sure he would drag her to the rabbi the next morning and divorce her in half an hour, or however long it took. He wouldn't even give her what was due her from her marriage contract — since he didn't possess a thing himself. And so on the morning after the divorce she would be as miserable as Basha the agunah, whose husband had abandoned her and who went from house to house with tear-filled eyes begging to wash laundry, pluck geese, or knead dough.

Chiyene began to shiver. She looked through the little windows of the women's section into the men's section. Leybe stood next to his seat, his prayer shawl thrown nonchalantly over his shoulders. He patted his little black beard with satisfaction and seemed to smile.

He's still quite young, Chiyene thought, looking at him. He'd marry a young girl.

This thought struck her like a blow and she backed away from the little windows as though it had just thundered.

"Here are the glasses." Chiyene turned to the rebbetzin and quickly pulled the glasses from her nose, as if she wanted to save herself from terrible danger.

"So, God willing, will you buy a pair of glasses tomorrow?" the rebbetzin asked anxiously.

"No, rebbetzin. This will pass," Chiyene stammered with fright. "I'm only thirty-eight. It's still too early. . . . My husband sees quite well. . . . I'll see a doctor. . . . People say there are drops for the eyes. I want so much, dear rebbetzin, not to be like a grandmother at such a young age. . . . I don't want that. . . ."

Suddenly Chiyene stopped talking, as if she'd uttered some awful nonsense.

The rebbetzin stared at her wide-eyed, shook her head, and sighed, "Ah, sinful women . . ."

SHUT IN

LEYBELE WAS A ten-year-old lad with pale cheeks, black, moist, dreamy eyes, and small curly locks of black hair. Of course, his hair could be seen only when his little cap fell off his head, since Leybele was a pious lad who would never go bareheaded.

Leybele liked lots of things but he either never got them or never had them whole. That's why his eyes were always dreamy, worried, and brimming with yearning.

He loved the summer — but all day long he sat in cheder. He loved the sun — but his teacher always hung his gaberdine on the window, which made the room so depressingly dark. Leybele liked the moon and the night — but at home they closed the shutters and in bed he felt as if he were buried alive.

How strange were the ways of the world! He couldn't understand it. One would think that sunshine through a window was good, grand, and joyful. So the teacher blocks it out. No more sun. Leybele didn't have the nerve to ask, "Rabbi, what do you care if the sun shines through the window? How does it harm you?"

But Leybele would never ask. For the rebbi, so big and wise, no doubt had good reason. Then why did it seem to Leybele that it wasn't right? It must be because he was still so young. When he grew up perhaps he too would block the windows. But Leybele was still offended and always felt humiliated by adults.

Toward evening he returned home from cheder. The sun had already set and the street was astir with life and fun. Black beetles buzzed in flight and bumped into his nose, ear, and forehead. He would have liked to play outside awhile and forget about supper at home, but he was afraid of his father. Father was actually quite good-natured; with strangers he was gentle and friendly, but to Leybele he was very mean. He always yelled at him, and if Leybele came home a few minutes late from cheder, Father would immediately fly into a rage.

"And where have you been, my fine fellow? What business do you have out there?"

How could one explain to Father that it was so beautiful outside now? That he loved the buzzing of the beetles, that it was a pleasure listening to them? Even the way they bumped into his face as they flew by was nice and friendly too.

It all seemed absurd and foolish. Leybele enjoyed all these things because he was just a little boy — but Father was a grown-up who dealt with wheat and corn and always knew when the price was high and when it was low. He spoke Russian, could drive a bargain, and knew the Prussian scales. Father was really something! So how could Leybele tell his father that it was so nice outside now?

That's why Leybele hurried home after school. When he returned Father asked him how many chapters of Bible he had learned. When he replied, "Five," his father fell silent, hummed a little tune, and avoided his son's face. But if Leybele said, "Four," Father became angry.

"How come so few, huh?"

Leybele felt guilty and would not reply.

Then Father would ask him to translate a word from Hebrew.

"What does *kimeluneh* mean?"

"Kimeluneh means 'like a place to spend the night,' " said Leybele, frightened.

Father didn't say a word — a sign he was pleased. Then they sat down to supper, where Father constantly watched Leybele and taught him how to eat.

"Is that the way to hold a spoon?" he remarked drily. Leybele held it properly but didn't enjoy the meal.

After eating, Leybele had to say the Grace After Meals out loud and articulate the Hebrew correctly. If he swallowed a word Father would begin to yell.

"How did you say that? How? Say it again: 'You feed and sustain us . . .' Go ahead, say it! Don't rush, don't fly. . . . There's no fire. . . ."

Leybele repeated the phrase slowly even though he *was* in a rush, even though he *wanted* to fly outside, even though there *was* a great fire burning in him.

Darkness fell and Leybele recited the Evening Prayer by the light of the lamp. Father constantly caught him making mistakes and Leybele found it very difficult to keep from making more. The moon, clear and round, floated in the sky. Leybele looked at it while praying, felt the pull of the outdoors, and became flustered as he recited.

After prayers he gave some kind of excuse and slipped outside. He lingered awhile and looked up at the moon, which covered the street with pale rays of light. But soon he heard his father's voice: "Into the house to sleep."

It was warm outside. There wasn't even a breeze, but it seemed to Leybele that Father's words had created a wind. He felt an odd sensation of cold coming over him and returned to the house as if frozen. He stood by the window, gazing at the moon.

When he heard his father saying, "Well, it's time to close the shutters! No sense just sitting there," a wave of terror came over Leybele.

Father entered and Leybele could hear the banging of the shutters. He sensed their resistance, as though they were being closed against their will. Then one loud bang, and there was no more moon.

Father had hidden it.

A short while later the lamp was extinguished and the house was dark. Now everyone was asleep. Only Leybele, who lay by the window, could not fall asleep. Beckoning calls seemed to come through the cracks in the shutters. He would have liked to continue playing outside. He tried to sit up, to peep through the cracks. He even tried to open a shutter softly and gaze, just gaze outside, but he couldn't do it. Just then Father woke up and shouted, "What are you poking around over there for? Want me to whip you with the strap?"

And Leybele cuddled softly into his pillow, pulled the blanket over his head, and felt as if he'd been buried alive.

THE FREE LOAN

THE BIGGEST FAIR in Klemenke was the Ulas Fair, for which the shtetl always waited with a beating heart and great anticipation.

"Ulas is a God-send," the town's shopkeepers and dealers would say. "If not for the Ulas Fair, Klemenke would have gone under long ago and America would long ago have claimed the few Jews that are left here."

But for Ulas, one had to have something tangible in hand. The shopkeepers had to have goods, and the dealers — money. Without these Ulas too was nothing.

The fair was just three days away, but Chaim the grain dealer was walking about like a dead man, since he didn't even have a kopeck to buy grain.

Grain dealers swarmed around the marketplace, cheap cigarettes dangling from their mouths. Holding walking sticks and with cap brims askew, they spoke only about the fair.

"Exactly three days from now," said one.

"Imagine!" cried another. "In just three days things will break."

In market lingo "things will break" meant that big crowds were expected.

Chaim turned pale. He would even have prayed for some catastrophe to befall the fair — let it rain, snow, or storm that day, so that not even a mad dog would show up. But Chaim knew that the Ulas Fair wasn't like a frightened child. Ulas didn't fear even the worst blizzard. Ulas remained Ulas.

Chaim was at his wit's end. A free loan! Where could he get a loan? Even twenty-five rubles would do.

He asked around, but everyone answered with a cheerful snicker: "Are you mad? Crazy! Asking for money before a fair!"

And Chaim felt that he would indeed go mad.

"How about asking Leybe Beress?" Chaim's wife suggested, sharing his anguish.

"I thought about that too," Chaim replied, absorbed in thought.

"So?" his wife asked.

But I don't have the courage to go to him, Chaim wanted to say. However, since it was beneath his dignity to be so candid with his wife, he said, "Let him go to hell. He won't lend."

"But it doesn't hurt to try," she said, attempting to persuade him.

Chaim realized that he had no other choice. Leybe Beress was a rich man; he lived up the street and they were neighbors. Since Leybe Beress was a timber merchant he didn't need ready cash now for the fair.

"Take out my Sabbath greatcoat," Chaim resolutely told his wife.

"Right you are!" she said. "Going to see him is the best move."

Chaim stood before the half-broken little mirror nailed to the wall. He smoothed his beard with both hands, tucked his earlocks behind his ears, then removed his hat and brushed it with his sleeve.

"See if the back of my jacket is dusty. I may have rubbed against a whitewashed wall."

"So you did," his wife replied and began to swat his shoulders with both hands.

"I think we once had a little clothes brush. Where is it?"

"You must be dreaming!" Slapping his shoulders, his wife said softly, "You really got yourself full of dust, didn't you?"

"All right, enough banging!" Chaim's shout bordered on anger. "I'm going . . ."

"May he have an extra year for every ruble he lends," Chaim muttered, donned his Sabbath greatcoat with a sigh, and left the house.

On his way to Leybe Beress, Chaim's heart trembled. During the years that the rich man had lived at the end of the street, Chaim had been to his house only twice, and he considered this visit a kind of test. The entrance to the house, the bright rooms, the big mirrors, the plush furniture, all frightened him. And Leybe Beress with his long wide beard and the stern eyes of a rich man scared him too. And so did his wife, his lively, happy children, and even the maid whom Chaim remembered from the previous two visits.

"Where are you going? Are you crazy? Turn back!" a voice in his head seemed to be saying, and every few moments Chaim would stop dead in his tracks. But he was prompted to continue by the thought that the Ulas Fair would soon begin and he didn't have a kopeck to buy grain and rent space in the granary.

Leybe Beress won't lend. There's no need to get my hope up in vain, Chaim thought as he walked, preparing himself for the blow. Nevertheless, he realized that such pessimism would prevent him from even opening his mouth and articulating his request.

If Leybe Beress is in a good mood, he consoled himself, he'll lend me the money. Why should he be afraid of lending me a few rubles till after the fair? I'll tell him that as soon as I sell the grain I'll repay the loan. I'll swear by the life of my wife and children. He'll believe me. And of course, I *will* return the money. . . .

But these thoughts did not boost Chaim's confidence, and he sought another consolation, another approach to raise his spirits.

He's not a bad man, Chaim thought. And besides, we didn't just meet yesterday. We've been living on the same street for twenty years.

And Chaim recalled that two weeks ago Leybe Beress had passed Chaim's little house just when he, Chaim, was out in the yard. He had greeted Leybe Beress cordially, as befitted a rich man (I could swear I shook his hand, Chaim tried to remember), and Leybe Beress had responded amicably too. He had even stopped and, like a good acquaintance, asked him, "How are you doing, Chaim?"

Chaim tried to recall his reply and remembered saying, "Thanks for asking. Thank God, fine. I'm doing business."

I answered him quite self-assuredly, Chaim thought, pleased with his response.

So Chaim decided that now he would also talk to Leybe

Beress with greater self-assurance and pride. To flounder or fall — never!

Chaim looked up and saw Leybe Beress's house in the distance. He coughed to clear his throat, smoothed his beard, and contemplated his greatcoat.

"It's still in quite good shape," he said out loud to perk up his courage and self-esteem.

But walking up to Leybe Beress's big house, with its sparkling lights glinting from the eight large windows, Chaim felt his heart flutter.

"O God Almighty, help me!" The unwitting cry rose from deep within him. But at once he felt ashamed and stood fast. "Oh, nonsense!"

As he pulled the door open, a more passionate prayer tore out of him: "Help me, Almighty God! My blood is running cold. . . ."

At a large table covered with a clean tablecloth, Leybe Beress sat drinking tea and talking gaily with his family. The rich man's twelve-year-old son saw Chaim standing by the door and called, "A man has come, Papa."

"Yes, it's a man," a second son shouted merrily, gazing at Chaim with his big mischievous black eyes.

The group around the table began staring at Chaim. Another minute, he thought, and I'm going to collapse. But he braced himself, thinking how it would be if he fell down. Then, without as much as a "Good evening," Chaim took another step and stammered, "I happened to be passing by, you see, and saw you sitting here . . . which meant, of course, that you were home . . . so . . . I thought to myself, well, I ought to drop in . . . neighbors, after all. . . ."

"By all means, with pleasure." Leybe Beress smiled amiably. "You're a welcome guest. Why don't you sit down?"

As Chaim heard the response, a stone rolled off his heart and, looking at the two boys, he slipped timorously into a chair.

"Leah!" The rich man summoned the maid. "Bring Reb Chaim a glass of tea!"

He's such a nice man, Chaim thought, looking gratefully at Leybe Beress. May God be good to him! And Chaim wanted to embrace the rich man's thick neck and kiss him.

"Well, how are things with you?" Leybe Beress asked.

"Thank God! I'm coming along."

The maid brought Chaim a glass of tea. He thanked her but immediately regretted it. Thanking a servant wasn't in good taste. He flushed and bit his lips.

"Put some preserves in the tea," Leybe Beress suggested.

Leybe Beress's generous demeanor took Chaim by surprise. What a dear soul! What a precious man, he thought. Now he'll surely lend me the money.

"Are you doing any business?" the rich man asked.

"Of course," Chaim replied confidently. "I'm trading no less than the other merchants."

"What's the current price for oats?" Leybe Beress asked.

The price of oats had fallen lately, but Chaim felt it would be better to say it had risen.

"It's moved quite high," Chaim declared with the tone of a merchant.

"Well, and do you have a supply of oats in stock?" the rich man asked, pursuing his inquiry.

"I've got quite a nice supply. I didn't pay much for it. Bought it quite cheap, in fact," Chaim answered with increased passion, forgetting that it had been several weeks since he'd had a grain of oats in the granary.

"And do you have the funds to speculate?" Leybe Beress asked. "You don't need any money?"

"Thank God," Chaim answered proudly, "I never lacked money."

What am I saying? Chaim thought, frightened by his own words. Oh, woe is me! How can I ask him for a loan now? And Chaim wanted to reverse course, to pull the wagon back, but Leybe Beress interrupted him.

"Which means you're doing good business. You must be fairly well off . . ."

May my enemies be so fairly well off, Chaim wanted to say. But looking at the rich man's shining face and at the blue crock of preserves on the table, Chaim answered proudly, "Thank God, I have nothing to complain about."

There goes your free loan! The thought hit Chaim like a blow in the back of the head. You jackass! Idiot! What are you bragging about? Tell him that you need twenty-five rubles for the Ulas Fair. Let him save you. Tell him that you're going under . . . that —

But the more he spoke the more upbeat Chaim's tone became; he kept bragging about his business deals and passed the time with the rich man as though he were his equal.

Soon, however, Chaim felt he was superfluous here. He sensed he shouldn't have sat down at the table or spoken in this manner. He should have spoken about the fair, about the loan . . . But now it was too late. "I don't need any money."

With despairing glances Chaim looked at Leybe Beress's cheerful face and at his two sons, who sat opposite him. The boys watched Chaim with roguish amusement, exchanging strange whispers and even more peculiar smiles.

A cold sweat drenched Chaim. He stood.

"Are you leaving already?" Leybe Beress asked politely.

The thought that he could still save himself crossed Chaim's mind; perhaps now I can ask him. But looking at the two lads who were watching him with their sly and mischievous eyes, Chaim answered regally, "I have to go! Business! No time!"

On his way to the door it seemed to Chaim that the two boys with the mischievous eyes gave him a fico behind his back, sticking their tongues out at him too, while Leybe Beress smiled and encouraged them: "Give it to him! Bigger ones!"

Chaim felt that his back was on fire and he quickly left the house.

MATZA
FOR THE RICH

THE OWNER OF the bakery entered her shop in a dither.
"After this order is done," she declared, "we will bake
Feige Chana's flour."

The women who rolled the dough stood stock still as if
stuck to the baking boards. They were so astonished they
couldn't say a word. Only one man, who perforated the
dough with a little scoring wheel, had the courage to repeat,
"Feige Chana?"

"Yes! Feige Chana! She'll be here in a couple of hours."

One of the dough rollers, Gruneh, the teacher's wife,
turned to her fellow workers. Her face was shining with joy.

"From her we'll get a really big tip."

"Yes, oh yes," many voices agreed. "Such a rich lady is
no small matter!"

A buzz ran through the bakery. Everyone was predicting
how much money the wealthy Feige Chana would distribute
among the workers.

"And I tell you," said Freyde, Berl the tailor's wife, "that
she won't give us more than anybody else. Feige Chana is
known to be tightfisted."

"If Freyde talks it must be worth hearing," Gruneh said with a touch of sarcasm. "It's true that Feige Chana is no big giver; still, it wouldn't be fitting for a rich lady like her to give the bakers any less than three rubles."

"Seeing is believing," joked the young, pale dough scorer.

At this point, Chaim the baker could no longer contain himself. Throughout the excitement he had worked diligently as if it were no concern of his. He draped the thin, rolled-out circles of dough over a long stick and inserted them into the oven. Then, holding a couple of dry matzas, he turned to the women.

"Be happy," Chaim said in a voice full of irony and pessimism. "Be merry and glad, children. You'll thank God if you escape her claws alive. Feige Chana is going to torment the life out of you. One batch of matzas she'll say is too big; another she'll criticize for being too thick. About a third batch she'll complain they're too meagerly perforated . . . or burnt."

Chaim already seethed with anger and stopped speaking, convinced that what he had predicted was precisely what would happen. He went to the oven and, nabbing a couple of matzas with the inserting stick, continued: "I know her. Let her go to hell. I hate those rich people's guts."

At the word "rich" Chaim purposely spat, like a pious Jew during the *Alenu* prayer.

For a short while, Chaim's enraged voice and venomous remarks were greeted with silence by all the workers. Yankeleh, a little orphan boy who poured the flour onto the baking boards for the dough rollers, stood by the flour sack, his small black eyes popping with astonishment. Dusted with flour and white as a ghost, he seemed to be pleading with Chaim: Don't frighten me! I'm scared!

But Gruneh, the teacher's wife, didn't change her mind. She still thought that the rich lady would leave a nice tip. In fact, anticipating that Feige Chana would approach and tell her to roll the dough out thinner, Gruneh had already prepared a response: "May you eat in good health!" she would say. "I'm rolling it as thin as I can."

And she would articulate her good wishes and thanks for the rich lady's tip by saying, "May you live and be well until next year!" Then she'd add in Hebrew, "Next year in Jerusalem!" Let the rich lady see, Gruneh thought, that she too knew how to express good wishes in a grand manner.

Meanwhile, Gruneh rolled out the dough, smiling all the while, as if she'd had a beautiful dream. Expecting a heap of good fortune, she felt a pleasant shiver roll through her heart. Feige Chana . . . a rich lady . . . three rubles . . . perhaps five. And her share would be thirty kopecks. She would buy a half-silk kerchief in honor of Passover.

The matza order that preceded the rich lady's was now finished. Soon they would bring Feige Chana's flour.

It was 3:00 P.M., a time when a new load of wood was added to the oven. Since heating it took an hour and a half, the dough rollers and the other workers could leave for a meal at home and a short rest that refreshed them for late-night work. But because of the rich lady, this time they ate quickly and returned at once to the bakery to prepare for Feige Chana's order.

"Scrape the dough boards and the rolling pins *very well*," came the owner's stern command. "And wash your hands thoroughly. Put on clean aprons and don't be vulgar when Feige Chana is here. And don't sing any ditties."

"All this fuss for one rich lady! It's crazy!" Chaim the baker spat out, even though he himself always complained about the women singing during work.

"No, it isn't," Gruneh the teacher's wife blurted, as if incensed. "Chaim thinks that Feige Chana is some plain nobody, like the other women."

"And you," the bakery owner turned to the young dough scorer, disregarding Chaim's remark, "don't joke with Tsipkele when she brings you a matza for the oven."

"Nonsense! What do you want from me?" cried Tsipkele, a young girl with disheveled black shoulder-length hair. "All of a sudden she's picking on me!"

The owner, apparently unfazed by Tsipkele's shouts, turned and chided her: "And it wouldn't hurt if you braided your hair when you work on the rich lady's matza. The dough scorer won't like you any less!"

The dough scorer wanted to respond but the owner ran to the door. There, however, she remembered something and ran right back to the oven. She stuck her head halfway in and, when she withdrew, asked Chaim anxiously, "Tell me, Reb Chaim, do you have enough dry wood?"

"Yes, I do, I do," he said, with mingled pride and vexation.

"Make absolutely sure!" The owner shook a warning finger at him and rushed out. She apparently still had many things to do pertaining to the rich lady's matza order.

Now the bakery came to life. The women scrubbed the baking boards and the rolling pins. The dough scorer chose his finest scoring wheel and inspected it for a possible flaw, for he didn't want the matzas to be torn apart. Gruneh ran around in a turmoil looking for a better rolling pin that would work the dough with greater ease. Spotting one just right for her under Freyde's arms, she began sweet-talking and cajoling her to make an exchange, but Freyde thanked her profusely for the favor and refused to hear of it. And Chaim the baker, his face flaming, swept the oven, afraid it might get too hot. He vented his rage at anyone who passed by and shouted, "Out of my way! Go to the devil along with her!"

Now the porter brought in the rich lady's flour. Everyone fell silent and regarded him with awe. When he carried other people's flour, he had to yell, "Watch it, let me through," but now a wide path opened up for him. The workers even regarded the sack of flour with respect. Gruneh approached, about to take a pinch of the meal to test its quality, but little Yankeleh, who poured the flour onto the baking boards, chased her away.

"Move!" the orphan lad cried proudly. "It's none of your business. It's the rich lady's flour."

Like the grown-ups, Yankeleh also sensed the change that had come over the bakery with Feige Chana's matza order. His little head, bent over the bag of flour, already reckoned the tip she would give him. For him this tip was more important than for any other baker, since he got no wages. His sole earnings came from tips.

"Well, as far as I'm concerned, she can come now!" Gruneh shouted suddenly. She had found a rolling pin she liked, just right for the rich lady's matza.

"So when is she coming?" everyone asked impatiently, fully prepared.

"She's already forgotten all about it," Chaim shouted angrily.

"Shh, she's coming," Tsipke the dough roller announced, looking out the window.

"What are you talking about?"

"Ha, ha, ha," Tsipke giggled. "Fooled you."

"Brazen witch!" Gruneh shouted. "You nearly gave me a heart attack."

"Why'd you get so scared, Gruneh?" Tsipke laughed.

"Me, scared? Not at all! But to shout like that?" Gruneh said, ashamed of her earlier remark.

"Shh, shh, as I live and breathe, she's really on her way," said another dough roller.

Everyone fell silent.

The door opened. The rich Feige Chana, a tall, heavy-set woman with a nicely rounded face and beautiful but harsh eyes, looked severely at the bakers as she entered.

"A good day to you ladies," she intoned like a general addressing his soldiers.

"Thank you, thank you," the dough rollers said twice — once in reply to her greeting and once more because she was a rich lady.

The bakery owner ran in, frightened that she had not noticed Feige Chana entering.

"There's so much work," she apologized, "no end of work. No small matter when you're dealing with matza. So please forgive me. Forgive me."

The rich lady did not reply, but approached to inspect the oven.

"I hope the baker isn't burning the matza," she said, turning to the owner even though Chaim was standing right there.

What's the matter? Chaim thought, hurt and fuming. Can't she ask me? Big shot! Chaim felt like cursing and in a fit of fury threw a piece of wood into the oven.

The owner, frightened by the rich lady's question, began to explain: "Oh my goodness! What are you talking about? What do you mean burning the matza? No one's matza is burnt here, especially yours. The matza comes out as if baked in the sun."

"Just remember that." Feige Chana smiled.

"What a question!" the owner said, pleased with the rich lady's smile.

Feige Chana walked over to the women who rolled the dough, followed by the owner, who winked at one of them. But the latter, not grasping what she meant, grew frightened.

"You're a fool!" the owner whispered into her ear, seeing that she could accomplish nothing with a wink. "Button up your jacket."

The baking began.

Gruneh, the teacher's wife, tried to position herself next to the rich lady. Perhaps she'd succeed in talking to her and telling her about her impoverished life — and then the rich lady would leave her a nicer tip of her own accord. Gruneh threw fawning glances at Feige Chana, looked her in the eye, smiled ingratiatingly, but didn't have the nerve to say a word. If she talks to me, I'll answer, Gruneh thought, and waited.

Feige Chana sat on a chair next to her load of dough and prepared the dough pellets. In order that her matzas be thinner she made small spheres of dough and handed them to the dough rollers. As she worked the dough with her rolling pin, she was on the lookout lest the women make one ball out of two. Assuming they must be doing this, she said angrily, "Women! Girls! Don't make one out of two!"

"Who?" All the women exchanged frightened glances.

"Maybe I'm wrong," Feige Chana said coldly. "But it just seemed to me . . ."

A pall of fear came over the dough rollers. Gruneh no longer had any intentions of talking to her. She thanked God that the rich lady wasn't pestering her. She tried to roll out the dough as best she could. When the matza came out well, she held it up on the rolling pin to show the rich lady how nice it looked.

Finally — heaven be praised! — the baking was done. All the workers, except for Chaim the baker, became more animated. What apprehension, what a load off their backs! The matzas came out "beautifully," as the owner expressed it. "Main thing," she said, "is to eat it in good health." She offered a couple of matzas to the rich lady and said with a smile, "See how they shine like a mirror?"

Feige Chana approached the bed where the matzas were placed when they emerged from the oven. She contemplated them, obviously looking to find fault, but she didn't readily succeed. That's why she had seemed displeased and was silent when the owner had praised the matza. Finally, the rich lady began to look more cheerful.

"The matzas were too skimpily perforated," she said.

A wave of fright rolled over the dough scorer. Turning pale, he explained to Feige Chana as politely as he could that it would have been impossible to make the perforations any deeper, since the matzas would have crumbled.

"If you wanted to, you could have done it," the rich lady replied.

The dough scorer was dumbstruck. Whether he was more vexed that his effort and hard work weren't appreciated, or insulted that the woman had addressed him — a man already twenty years old — in the familiar "you" form, it was hard to tell.

The porter took Feige Chana's matzas from the bed and placed them in large baskets woven of thin reeds. Although he was extremely careful not to break them, he wasn't successful. The matzas were so perfectly dry they broke in the basket.

"Bandit!" Feige Chana berated the porter. "I won't have a whole matza left for the Seder."

The small, hunched porter became even smaller and more bent over. He wanted to tell the rich lady that it wasn't his fault. But looking at her his blood curdled, his courage vanished, and he slowly and carefully arranged the matzas in the basket.

The repacking was completed. The two big baskets were full and the porter was ready to carry them as soon as the rich lady gave the word.

Feige Chana now began settling her account with the owner.

All the other workers in the bakery waited with pounding hearts. How much would she leave them? Aside from the fact that they were all poor and needed every kopeck, they were also curious about the size of the tip.

After paying the owner, Feige Chana began distributing money to the workers. She gave it out with a haughty air and as if she hadn't counted it. Good wishes and blessings surged sky high. Hopes for her to have millions flew left and right. A long, happy life. Good health. Joy from your children. But the good wishes that Gruneh had prepared earlier — "Next year in Jerusalem!" — remained unsaid. Somehow the opportunity hadn't presented itself. It would have been as insignificant as a cough during an illness, she thought. Never mind. Main thing is to have no more anguish.

As soon as the rich lady left the bakery, the question rang out: "How much? How much?"

Everyone quickly inspected the coins in their hands and complaints rose through the bakery.

"Oy, what a swine she is! She left only one ruble for the dough rollers. *One* ruble for eighteen women."

"Worth slaving for!"

"How carefully we turned and shaped her matzas."

"A rich lady's luck."

"What did I tell you?" Chaim the baker shouted. "That swine left me only fifteen kopecks."

"I didn't even get that much," the scorer complained. "She only slipped me a ten-kopeck coin."

"Inspect it. See if it isn't counterfeit." Chaim laughed.

"Listen, children," the bakery owner interjected like a friend, "this is the first time she's baked matza with me and I hope it's the last. I don't make any money on her. During the time her matzas were baking I could have done two customers. And she only paid me fifteen kopecks more per forty pounds of flour. And if you believe her, you'd think she'd overpaid me!"

A spirited mood now pervaded the bakery. All the workers criticized Feige Chana. Puns and jokes flew in the air, and the owner beamed with joy.

Everyone praised Chaim the baker. "He's really smart," they said. "He predicted this right from the beginning!"

The compliment pleased Chaim. Of course! he thought. The rich have the money and I have the brains. He wanted to say something, but the sudden sound of someone crying broke through the chatter.

"Shh! Who's crying?" everyone wondered. The workers looked around and noticed that in a corner, with his head against the wall, stood little Yankeleh — the orphan who poured the flour onto the kneading boards — weeping bitterly, rubbing his wet eyes with his hand and smearing his face.

"Why are you crying, Yankeleh? What's the matter?"

"She . . . didn't . . . leave . . . me . . . anything," the little boy sobbed.

"Oh, may a plague wrack her!" tore out of everyone's mouth.

"Just as she forgot about this little orphan, so may God forget about her children," others cursed.

The maledictions were grim and deeply felt. Looking at the workers as they reviled the rich lady, one could see that they would have been delighted to have every one of their curses come true.

"How come you didn't go up to her yourself, you fool?" the owner reproved him softly.

"I was afraid of her," the little orphan wailed.

"You're not afraid of anyone, except her!" she continued to chide the boy. "If you see her giving to everyone but you, you go up to her and say, 'Excuse me, but you forgot me.' . . . It's only natural."

While the owner spoke, Chaim the baker stood staring straight ahead with bloodshot eyes. He raised his clenched fists over his head as if he wanted to beat himself. But when the little orphan boy burst into even more grievous weeping after the owner had stopped speaking, Chaim approached him, stroked his little head, and attempted a smile.

"Don't cry, little silly. She left me five kopecks for you.

Here!" And saying this, he slipped the money into the boy's hand.

The women workers looked on. Gruneh, the teacher's wife, was about to make a snide remark: "A pauper becomes a philanthropist!" But looking at the orphan's tear-stained face, she couldn't manage to utter a word.

"O God Almighty!" she sighed softly. "Why should the rich have everything?"

HOLY BOOKS

NOTTE SHYKESS, a well-to-do shtetl householder who earned a living from moneylending and a dry-goods store managed by his wife, returned from the bes medresh pleased and in high spirits.

After the morning service he had engaged the rabbi in a bit of a Talmudic dispute. The rabbi had resolutely held to his view, but Notte Shykess couldn't easily be dissuaded either, and it was he who emerged victorious. Notte had proved his point by showing the rabbi that the law in question was explicitly cited in the Talmud.

But he couldn't share this with his wife, Zlateh. First of all, what does a woman know of these matters? And secondly, she was already busy with the Sabbath preparations. On Friday, business in his dry-goods shop was slow and the hired girl could tend to the customers by herself.

"Why are you so late?" Zlateh said as she turned to him.

"It's nothing." Notte waved his hand disparagingly.

"Set the table, Golde," Zlateh said to her elder daughter who stood bent over the potatoes, peeling them for the Sabbath cholent. Ever since Zlateh had begun to manage her own household, she had been using potatoes for the cholent.

Golde set the table and brought a pale roll for her father. After Notte had washed his hands and said the prayer over bread, he went to the big bookcase and took out a small sacred text entitled *Yodov Emuna*. He sat, chewed the roll, and read, a habit he'd acquired over the years. He had to peruse a holy book while eating; otherwise, he didn't enjoy his meal.

Turning a few pages, Notte noticed that the book was dusty and emitted a musty smell.

It's been a long time since we aired out the books, he chided himself. It's a nice day, and there's a breeze too. Yes, we'll bring the books out right now to be aired.

After breakfast he announced his decision. "Children!" he shouted gaily. "Help me air out the holy books!"

"Air out the holy books! Air out the holy books!" echoed throughout the house. All at once, everyone started running in all directions, like soldiers in a barracks, just before the division doctor makes an inspection. But this was a merrier, more spirited tumult.

"Papa!" the youngest son, Aron, cried out joyfully. "We have to bring a bench to the yard to put the books on, right?"

"Of course, of course," the father agreed, stroking the edges of his beard.

"Chiyeneh!" Areleh turned to his little sister with a bossy tone. "Help me with the bench. Papa has to air out the holy books."

As the two children hastily dragged out the bench, they knocked over the long, crooked oven poker, which fell on Zlateh's foot. But she wasn't upset; on the contrary, her heart was filled with respect and awe for the holy procession. She didn't dare say a word.

The father followed the children and showed them where to place the bench, then sent them back to the house for the books.

The children began to carry the enormous set of the linen-bound Talmud with both hands.

"One at a time," Notte suggested. "You'll get exhausted."

"Don't worry, Papa!" Aron shouted with joy. "Come, Chiyeneh, let's get more."

Notte arranged the books on the long bench so that the wind could air out the pages. The wind boldly took to the mitzva, turning the pages back and forth. The wind, it seemed, was a great Talmudic scholar. Now it was reading the opening section of "He who places his pitcher . . ." and a moment later it was already up to the chapter "He who sells a ship . . ." Then suddenly the wind had a notion to study the entire volume all at once and it turned all the pages to and fro, from side to side.

Aron and little Chiyeneh kept bringing their father more books: the Shulkhan Arukh, the Tur, a commentary by Moses Alshikh, and Ye'aros Dvash. The wind studied them all diligently and turned one page after another as Notte stood by, watching proudly.

"Bring more, more," he told the children.

"I know!" said Aron excitedly, out of breath from the great effort. "There's plenty more. Three more shelves. Come, Chiyeneh, let's bring another bench."

The children brought out another bench that was immediately filled with smaller books, which Notte had bought from itinerant book peddlers for fifteen, ten, and even, on occasion, five kopecks.

The wind didn't snub the little books either. It turned their pages quickly and accepted them along with the larger ones, as if for the wind they were all the same, all containing Torah learning.

The wind turned the pages noisily.

Notte stood contemplating the books. When the children brought two ancient, dusty tomes without covers, he asked, "Is that it, children?"

"No more." Aron made a broad gesture with his little hand.

"No more," Chiyeneh agreed shyly.

"Well, then, go into the house," Notte said genially.

"Oh, Papa, I'd like to stand here and watch," Aron pleaded.

"Me too watch," Chiyeneh pleaded like her brother.

"All right, then, stay," their father said.

As the children stood there with shining eyes, Notte heard Zlateh calling.

"Areleh! I think Mama is calling you."

"Aron! Aron!" came Zlateh's voice.

"What is it?" Aron was annoyed at his mother's summons. He didn't want to leave this fine show — the pages fluttering, airing out, turning quickly back and forth.

"Go, my son, she needs you for something. You can come right back," the father said.

Areleh entered the house disgruntled.

"What do you need me for, Mama?"

Zlateh braced herself to say something very difficult.

"Come, say it already," Areleh urged her.

"Go, my son, and fetch my Yiddish Bible from the dark alcove. It's on the little table. Take it and air it out a bit too."

"It doesn't have to be done to a Yiddish Bible," Areleh snapped authoritatively.

Zlateh blushed and gave a sad smile. "Silly boy! A Yiddish Bible is also a holy book."

But she didn't really believe her own words.

"Go. Take it. . . ." Her voice broke and she barely managed to conclude, "and bring it outside."

Aron obeyed his mother. He entered the dark little room and took the Yiddish Bible. As he was about to leave, Zlateh thought it over and stopped him: "You're right. It's not necessary."

Aron looked at his mother and sensed that she had become sad. He felt sorry for her and, affected by her mood, said, "No, I'll air it out."

"Well, then," Zlateh said hesitantly, "take it outside if you wish." She walked to the window, looked into the yard, and listened with pounding heart.

"What did you bring now?" Notte asked.

"Mama's Yiddish Bible," Aron shouted with a laugh.

"Really?" Notte too laughed affably. "She wants to air out her holy books too. Well, nothing wrong with that. With pleasure!"

Zlateh watched as Notte held the Yiddish Bible and turned the pages. Then, with a smile, he placed it among the big, thick holy books.

"Oh, why did I insist on doing this?" Zlateh reproached herself, seeing the wind turn the pages of her Yiddish Bible.

Every once in a while, the pages of her favorite stories, like "Rachel Tending Her Sheep" or "Miriam and Her Drum," fluttered by.

Zlateh sadly thought how unpleasant a task this must be for Notte. She deeply regretted her foolish deed: letting her son take her women's Yiddish Bible to air out with so many of the men's holy books.

THE
COUNTERFEIT COIN

AFTER MUCH EFFORT, Glicksman finally succeeded in getting private lessons at the homes of some rich families, which provided him with a livelihood during the winter. But now that the families had dispersed to their summer residences, he remained in the big city without a kopeck to his name and with no hope of getting any work till the following winter.

Among his friends Glicksman was considered an honest and diligent young man who wanted to be productive but had nowhere to direct his energies. Despite their own poverty, at first his friends supported him with their last kopecks, which they would give him as "loans."

After each such "loan" Glicksman felt humiliated and repeatedly promised himself that as soon as he got his first tutoring job he would gratefully repay everyone.

However, several weeks passed and his impoverished friends became even poorer, while yet more unemployed tutors were added to their ranks. Glicksman's friends grew accustomed to his situation and it seemed that starvation was to be his lot.

He envisioned the hunger and it frightened him like a dark apparition, but he continued to struggle and seek ways to avoid his plight. The first antidote was to swallow his pride, a step that wasn't planned in advance. It simply happened on its own and Glicksman didn't even feel its demeaning aspects.

Soon, Glicksman stopped promising himself that as soon as he got his first private lesson he would thank his friends and repay all his debts. Now he racked his brains with a more important question: Where could he borrow some money for food? As for repaying, let God worry about that!

With the passing days Glicksman increasingly humbled himself and pleaded pitifully to borrow a few kopecks. To add punch to his request, he would often blurt, "Believe me, I haven't had breakfast yet."

Later, he would spit a few times as if he'd swallowed something disgusting. Once he even slapped himself angrily and shouted, "You're begging!" But as soon as he encountered someone else he knew, his hunger prompted him to repeat the humiliating phrase with increased ardor, force, and pathos.

The next time Glicksman was refused, he accepted it with greater equanimity; he didn't slap himself but sighed with self-pity and sought out a third, a fourth, and a fifth acquaintance.

It was twelve noon, and the street was bustling with people. Glicksman walked through the crowd searching for something with his ravenous eyes. He felt that this great mass of people moving to and fro, pedestrians and riders alike, were all brothers hustling and bustling, running and pursuing, everyone earning a livelihood and with a place to eat. But him — he didn't know why — they had cast out of this brotherhood, and because they refused to give him a share he would expire of hunger.

He felt humiliated in the presence of the passersby and ashamed for himself as well. He was young and educated; he had hands willing to work, feet to run wherever needed, and a head capable of logical thought. And a young man like him was walking about on the street in broad daylight helpless and hungry! How disgraceful! How repulsive!

The more he walked the hungrier and weaker he became. His knees buckled. He felt dizzy and he was scared he might fall. In despair, he sought words of consolation to fortify himself and regain strength to struggle and remain alive.

I'm not alone! He repeated the only thought that would comfort him. There are many here like me!

He looked everyone he met in the face, as though he wished to find someone like himself. But all the faces seemed so sated and contented that his despair only increased. He walked on and on without knowing where or why.

Suddenly, he saw the flash of a familiar hat and then a face: an acquaintance with whom he'd exchanged a few words two or three times; he wasn't even sure of his family name.

He'll lend, flew through Glicksman's head, and he stopped the man with a dispirited "Good morning."

Glicksman's acquaintance stared as if he didn't remember him.

"Have you forgotten?" Glicksman asked ingratiatingly. "We met at Silberman's, remember? I'm Glicksman."

"Aha!" his acquaintance recalled with a smile but said nothing more.

Again, the thought raced through Glicksman's head: He'll lend!

"Do you know why I stopped you?" he stammered. "My place isn't too far from here. . . . I need a few kopecks quite badly and I forgot my wallet at home. Can you lend me twenty kopecks till tomorrow or the day after tomorrow at the latest? You must do it!"

Instead of replying, the man put his hand into his pocket. Glicksman's heart began pounding rapidly.

"You see?" the man said, opening and shaking his coin purse.

A black curtain descended before Glicksman's eyes. The purse was empty.

"Oy!" A despairing groan tore out of him. Embarrassed at having moaned like that, he barely managed to say, "You don't have to show me. I believe you."

"I do have a forty-kopeck coin in one of my pockets, but it's counterfeit," the acquaintance added, as if he wanted to distract Glicksman from his embarrassment.

Glicksman brightened. "Let's have a look." As his acquaintance searched his pockets, he kept cautioning Glicksman that he had surely thrown the coin away. Glicksman waited, terror-stricken.

"Wait! I found it!" the man announced.

"Let's see! Let me see it!" Glicksman practically tore the forty-kopeck coin from the man's hand.

As he contemplated the coin carefully, his heart sank. It was as yellow as brass and light as tin, but somehow Glicksman couldn't give it back.

"Give it to me," he said, "perhaps I'll . . ."

"Oh, take it." The acquaintance perked up as if delighted to be rid of the yellow coin.

"Adieu," Glicksman said, avoiding the other man's face. He felt his own face burning with shame as if it had been doused with kerosene and set alight.

Angry at himself for what he had done, Glicksman petulantly decided to spend the forty kopecks.

"I must spend it," he shouted so loudly that a couple of passersby turned to stare.

With his heart beating wildly, Glicksman entered the first grocery he saw.

As a teacher, Glicksman was nicely dressed and with his pale, gentle face and delicate features, he looked like a well-to-do young man. Seeing him enter, the grocer stood and asked politely, "May I help you, sir?"

Glicksman nervously surveyed the few loaves of white bread and the great round of cheese on the counter and scarcely had enough strength to utter, "Two pounds of bread and a quarter pound of cheese." Then, in his agitation, he added, "Is the cheese good?"

"Choice cheese! Excellent! Made out of pure cream!" The grocer enthusiastically praised his wares. "Here, taste a piece. No harm."

And, while talking, the grocer offered Glicksman a piece of cheese from the tip of his knife.

Glicksman swiftly nabbed the cheese sliver and put it in his mouth. Recalling the yellow forty-kopeck piece, however, his hands and feet began trembling and he swallowed the cheese without even tasting it.

"An exquisite cheese," Glicksman managed to whisper, looking at the door as if wanting to flee.

"A quarter pound of cheese and two pounds of bread?" the grocer asked.

"A quarter pound of cheese and two pounds of bread," the flustered Glicksman repeated, wondering how he could slip the grocer the yellow coin without his noticing it.

The shopkeeper weighed the items, wrapped them in paper, and politely handed the package to Glicksman.

Hands shaking, Glicksman tossed the coin to the grocer.

"Give me change," he gasped and watched anxiously as the grocer grimaced while examining the coin.

"Excuse me!" The man turned to Glicksman after having bounced the coin three times and listening to its dull sound like a great composer. "Excuse me, but do you perhaps have another forty-kopeck piece? This one is counterfeit."

"Counterfeit?" Glicksman wondered with feigned innocence.

"Counterfeit," the grocer said frostily.

Glicksman returned the wrapped bread and cheese, took back the false coin, and inspected it from all sides.

"It's a perfectly good coin and I don't have another," he said quietly, and slipped out of the store like a shadow.

"What a great sale!" the grocer said sarcastically as he left. Glicksman felt the crumbs of cheese in his mouth and spat them out.

"What do I do now?" he groaned, wringing his hands and not knowing where to turn.

He looked at the coin in his hands.

"It's a perfectly good coin," he told himself, as if to talk himself into gathering up enough courage to enter another store.

But there too the same thing happened.

Glicksman left infuriated and embittered. His eyes were bloodshot. Evil beasts! he thought. Damn you all to hell! The humiliation made his blood boil and he looked with loathing at all the well-fed passersby.

I must spend the forty kopecks, he decided resolutely. I must! And he moved on.

He looked into every store he passed to see what kind of person sat behind the counter. But each of the shopkeepers' faces looked so gruff and mean that Glicksman's feet refused to carry him inside.

He was looking for a naive face or even a young child who could easily be fooled.

In a side lane he peered into a small shop. A thin little girl with a sleepy face and disheveled hair sat behind the counter, gazing sadly out to the street.

This is it! Glicksman thought and confidently strode in.

"Can I help you?" the little girl asked, seeing Glicksman casting wild glances at every corner.

Glicksman observed the girl's face; apparently she'd been crying.

One has to be a bandit to fool her, Glicksman said in his heart. But since hunger gnawed at him so painfully, he asked, "Do you have bread?"

"Yes," the little girl said, looking at him apprehensively.

She cut two pounds of bread. Glicksman noted her thin hands trembling as she sliced. Watching the poor child he felt a heavy load on his heart.

One has to be a bandit to fool her, his heart repeated with a force that almost overcame even his powerful hunger. He wanted to leave the store now, but the sight of the cut bread pulled him as though with tongs and he stayed.

"Give me a quarter pound of cheese too, little girl," he said weakly.

The girl weighed it and gave it to him.

"And give me change from forty kopecks." He handed her the coin, hoping in his heart that the poor child would have enough sense not to accept the false coin.

But the girl took it and, scarcely looking at it, threw it into a little box, and gave Glicksman ten kopecks change.

Glicksman broke into a cold sweat and couldn't leave the small shop.

"Little girl, do you have a mother?" Glicksman suddenly asked her.

"No, she died!" the girl answered sadly.

Glicksman almost collapsed.

"Do you have a stepmother?" he asked.

"Yes," she said even more gloomily.

"Does she hit you?"

The little girl didn't reply, but Glicksman was certain that the poor child was tormented daily. He imagined that for this counterfeit forty-kopeck piece her stepmother would beat her black and blue.

Glicksman nervously tapped the bread he held and, while looking at the walls of the humble shop and at the little girl, the words "One has to be a bandit to fool her," kept pounding in his head.

"Little girl," he suddenly shouted as if pleading. "I'm returning the bread and cheese. Give the forty-kopeck coin back to me."

"Why? Is the bread bad?" she asked apologetically.

"No. It's good bread. Excellent bread . . . but . . . listen to me, little girl . . . give me the forty-kopeck coin. Give it back, little girl."

The girl looked at him with astonished and frightened little eyes and returned the coin.

"A lovely little girl," he said gratefully. "In the future, little girl, inspect the coins you're given very carefully so you won't be fooled."

Without waiting for an answer, Glicksman ran out of the shop.

"I can't . . . I can't . . ." he justified his weakness. "I can't do it," he muttered and quickly flung the forty-kopeck coin to the cobblestones, where its dull clang mingled with his sigh.

And the famished Glicksman forged ahead, looking for someone he knew to lend him a few kopecks.

THE
POOR COMMUNITY

THE LITTLE SHTETL of Voinovke, which consisted of
thirty-five homes, swayed and roared and seethed like a
brook before Passover when the snow begins to thaw. But
it wasn't the eve of Passover. It was one week before Rosh
Hashana — and the community still didn't have a prayer
leader.

Nearby, in the much larger town of Yachnovke, one could
find a fine prayer leader who could do all the cantorial trills.
But a man like that wanted to be well paid — and herein lay
the tragedy! The shtetl had wasted its few rubles of communal funds on a cantor whom the devil himself had brought
into town during the past summer. Nevertheless, it was
worth hearing the cantor with his choir of six leading the
service on a Sabbath before the New Moon. Since the
founding of Voinovke, the shtetl hadn't heard such chanting.
The bes medresh, which according to the elders was more
than two hundred years old, barely survived the cantor and
his choir. The windows rattled, the walls shook, the plaster
fell from the ceiling.

Enraptured, they paid the cantor all the money the community possessed. Now, a week before Rosh Hashana, they realized that there wasn't a kopeck left to engage a prayer leader, and so the congregation assembled in the bes medresh to consider a solution.

"That was a foolish thing to do," shouted Aryeh Leib the tailor, who considered himself a pious Jew because he had a long beard and a young son who was studying in the Yachnovke yeshiva.

"Foolish isn't the word for it! A thing like that can happen only to us!" Chaim the glazier agreed. "Giving the cantor all our communal funds in the middle of the year!"

"It was insane! Absolutely crazy!" said Chonon the teacher, hunching his shoulders.

"You know what I'd recommend?" said Zerach the shoemaker as he stroked his beard with a rabbinic mien. "That those who hired the cantor should now hire a prayer leader with their own money. That's my suggestion," he concluded earnestly, as if everything depended solely upon his advice.

"Now go guess who hired him! Everyone hired him," said Zalmen the blacksmith, rejecting Zerach's advice. "Everyone wanted to hear some good cantorial singing for a change. Perhaps it's no crime. But when should this happen? When the shtetl is rich. Yachnovke can afford to spend money in midyear on a cantor, but not us beggars."

"So what's the decision?" came the shouts in the bes medresh.

"Things are pretty bad," someone said.

"Chaikl Sheps will lead us using Sabbath melodies," said Zerach the shoemaker, turning to the man who had conducted the Sabbath services. Chaikl Sheps had a fair voice, but the only prayer tunes he knew were Sabbath melodies.

"Come, Chaikl! Try it!" Some of the congregants turned to him. "Prepare yourself!"

Chaikl Sheps blushed and was barely able to say, "I'm scared."

"Try it! Try! *Ha-me-lech!*" Zalmen the blacksmith prompted him with a Rosh Hashana melody.

"So you know it yourself!" Chonon the teacher cried out and continued, "*Yo-shev-al-kisey-rom-ve-niso!*" And then the congregation began the traditional wordless ornamentation, "Ay . . . ay-ay . . . ay-ay . . ."

And for several minutes the bes medresh echoed with the High Holiday melodies that had so aroused the congregation.

"Everyone knows the melodies now," one of the men opined, "but at Rosh Hashana no one will remember a thing."

Everyone agreed, then fell into a deep reverie.

"We also don't have anyone to blow the shofar," the shamesh announced, standing in the pulpit.

The congregation was stunned.

"What do you mean? Where is Nachman?"

Nachman, a pale thin youth of twenty, came forward. He was fed by the villagers and studied on his own. For the past two Rosh Hashanas he had blown the shofar in the bes medresh without pay.

"This year I'm blowing the shofar in the village of Sosnovchineh. They're giving me three rubles . . . three rubles . . ." he barely managed to stutter, frightened because he had betrayed the community that fed him.

"What a rat you are!" someone shouted.

"Lowdown worm!" added another.

"Parasite!" came the insult from a third.

With all the abuse they heaped upon him, poor Nachman felt as if they were sticking him with needles.

"I have to have a winter coat made. I can't . . ." he pleaded. "Forgive me . . . It's very cold in the winter."

"What do you want from him?" The crowd backed down. "He needs a winter coat. He's going around naked, poor thing."

"That's true," everyone agreed.

"So now we haven't got a prayer leader or a man to blow the shofar."

"And I'm afraid we don't have anyone to read the Torah either," the shamesh said from the pulpit.

"What do you mean?" The congregation grew frightened. "Where is Alter Peshes? Where is he? Where?"

"Alter Peshes is also going to Sosnovchineh to read the Torah," Nachman said guiltily. "He's getting two rubles."

Now the congregation really became alarmed. Some lowered their heads as if searching for a solution; others stared up at the ceiling deep in thought for a few minutes.

"Never mind!" someone called out. "During these High Holidays we'll just have to pray individually . . . the community is finished!"

"What a turn of events!" One of the men laughed bitterly.

"This must be entered in the community register."

"Voinovke is finished!"

"Then let everyone chip in and hire someone with their own money," Chonon the teacher suggested and was immediately appalled by his own words.

"Come on, show me a ruble," said Zalmen the blacksmith, stretching out his hand.

"I don't have any," said Chonon, ashamed. "But there are householders who do."

"Who has money?"

"No one!"

"And the High Holidays are coming! It's no small thing."

"What's going to happen?"

"It's no good."

The bes medresh was abuzz. Every man had a different idea but none of the suggestions were any good.

Suddenly, the old shamesh banged the reader's desk and the crowd fell silent.

"Be still for a while," he said. "I have an idea."

"Let's hear it," everyone yelled impatiently.

The shamesh took a deeper breath than usual, helped himself to a big dose of snuff, wiped both sides of his nose, and finally said, "Here's the story. This past summer our community made a very foolish mistake. We wasted the few rubles we had on a little luxury. We forgot our poverty and our status and had a yen to hear a cantor — who he was, only the devil knows! An itinerant cantor is no saint. A truly pious cantor stays home. But be this as it may, the deed is done. The upshot is that now for the High Holidays we don't have a prayer leader, a shofar blower, or a Torah reader. We're down to nothing. And if you want to know something else, the shofar isn't in such great shape either. Now, in the month of Elul, somehow it still makes a few sounds. But when Rosh Hashana comes and we'll have to blow scores of notes — *teruah, shevorim, tekiah gedolah* — the shofar will surely get stuck. That's what happened last year, if you recall. . . . And Nachman blows the shofar very well."

The congregation looked at Nachman, who turned red.

"So my suggestion is," the shamesh continued, "that this year we should join the Sosnovchineh minyan. In other words, we should all go and pray with them. Walking is permitted. It's only about a mile and a half. So we'll take a stroll and spare ourselves the headache of where to get a prayer leader, a Torah leader, a shofar blower, and even a shofar. Because I tell you again, the shofar will refuse to function on Rosh Hashana. It won't take the rapid *teruah-shevorim* sounds. It can't. It's already old and has some defects. We have no choice but Sosnovchineh."

After the shamesh's speech the congregation began to clamor:

"From a town to a village? And on Rosh Hashana? No!"

"Let those villagers come to us!"

"Since when have they become such big shots?"

"Once upon a time those villagers used to come to us to pray."

"Now that they've learned to pray in Hebrew they make a minyan at home."

"Never mind the Hebrew. They sure know how to count money."

"They don't lack a thing! They have it all: bins full of potatoes, cabbage, chickens, and eggs."

"Cream, butter, and cheese."

"All our troubles on their heads."

"Shh, don't curse them! Jews, it's the month of Elul!"

The congregation became frightened of cursing in the month of Elul and backed down.

"Who's cursing? Who? Who?"

"No one. No one."

"What do we have against them?"

"Berke from Sosnovchineh is a good man. Praying at his place will be a pleasure. His house is as big as a field, three times the size of our bes medresh."

"Just this year he commissioned a scribe to write a Torah."

"A wonderful man!"

"And there's nothing wrong with the rest of the villagers. They're good people."

"Definitely."

"So the decision is — this Rosh Hashana we'll pray in Sosnovchineh."

"There's no other solution."

"It's a wonderful idea, I swear. A mountain's been removed from our shoulders."

"A mountain isn't the word for it."

"We'll have to ask Berke if he'll let us."

"Of course he'll let us! It'll be a great honor for him."

"No small matter! Shtetl Jews coming to pray in a village!"

And the meeting ended peaceably.

On the morning of the first day of Rosh Hashana, the shtetl Jews went to pray in Sosnovchineh (they had conducted the evening service at their own bes medresh the night before). As they passed their old, half-sunken bes medresh with its dimmed eyes, orphaned and forlorn, their hearts tugged and grieved, and with silent glances they begged its forgiveness.

TOO LATE

WITH THE HELP of his eighteen-year-old son, Sergei, Antosh had long ago threshed the little bit of corn he had harvested on the small parcel of land he owned. Then, in the nearby two-wheeled water mill, he had milled flour and stored it in the attic for bread in the winter. He had set aside only one forty-pound sack of cornmeal, tied it with a string, and brought it to the shtetl market. One Jew after another approached his wagon in the marketplace, felt the sack, and asked in Russian, "What are you selling?"

"Corn."

The Jews bargained and bargained, weighed it with their steelyards, and offered prices from forty kopecks to half a ruble. Antosh considered these offers, scratched the nape of his neck, and asked for seventy-five kopecks, which he finally dropped to sixty kopecks, or four gilden. He was obstinate about the latter price and no further bargaining availed.

"Four gilden," he insisted.

But toward evening, when the Jewish market merchants

had dispersed and no one came to him anymore, he dropped the price and looked for an offer of fifty kopecks.

Short Chonon, the only dealer left in the market, had already spent the bit of ready cash he'd set aside for purchases, so he halfheartedly offered forty-five kopecks. Since Antosh needed the money for necessities without which he couldn't return home, he agreed even though it caused him heartache. This bargain that would yield him a clean five-kopeck profit gave Chonon a jolt of joy in the right side of his heart, but in the left side he felt a stab of pain. How would he be able to take advantage of this bargain if all his capital had been used up during the day's activity in the market?

Nevertheless, Chonon lost neither hope nor faith and asked Antosh to bring the corn to his little granary. There, he struck a partnership with a richer dealer, who paid Antosh the three silver gilden. The peasant inspected the coins from all sides and asked several times if they were counterfeit. When the two partners assuaged his fears and told him the coins were perfectly good, Antosh slipped them deep into his chest pocket and rode off in his cart to an inn in the marketplace. There he tied his horse to a post of the porch and went in to buy the items he needed.

Antosh bought two pots of salt, which his wife had told him to bring without fail, three packages of cheap tobacco for four kopecks, a couple of pounds of soap for six kopecks, a wreath of bagels, and a small present for his little children. With the remaining money he entered the tavern, had a shot of whiskey, which refreshed him, and began to speak animatedly with the other peasants.

"I sold forty pounds of corn," he told one of them in his

tipsy state. "The Yids fooled me. Gave me only three gilden. Not enough!"

The other peasant, richer than Antosh, looked at him with contempt and said haughtily, "What's forty pounds of corn? I sold four hundred! You understand? Four hundred!"

Antosh looked enviously at the peasant. He wanted to respond, but his weak head was befuddled with drink. So he only grimaced and left the tavern with mingled feelings of joy and gloom. Then he climbed onto his small, open-sided cart and returned to his village three miles away.

A month passed. Autumn slipped in. The days became shorter, the nights longer. In Antosh's small house a lamp had to be lit at night. The clay jug that Antosh had bought from a potter three years before for four kopecks was dry and he had no money for kerosene. The salt was almost gone too: only a bit of soap remained and a two-day supply of tobacco. Antosh scratched the nape of his neck and spat.

"No salt, no soap, no tobacco," he grumbled. "Nothing. Bad business!"

Antosh had nowhere to turn to earn money. Berke, the only Jew in the village, was himself very poor. Antosh had only one hope: to cut a full wagon's worth of fir boughs before Sukkos, bring it to the shtetl, and sell it for eighty kopecks, which he had been doing every year since he had bought his horse for six rubles at a local fair.

Right after Rosh Hashana he asked Berke daily, "When is Sukkos?"

"You still have time," Berke would reply.

"But when is it?" Antosh persisted.

The Jew, distracted at the time, answered absently: "In about a week."

But in fact, it was only five days before Sukkos. And Antosh calculated that two days before Sukkos was the proper time to bring the fir boughs to the shtetl. That day happened to be the first day of the holiday.

That morning he rose early. He ate a piece of coarse black bread dipped into the salt he himself had pounded, drank a quart of cold water, harnessed his half-hungry, half-sleepy horse, took his hatchet, and went into the nearby forest.

He chopped the prickly branches of the fir trees and gathered the thickest and the longest. Better merchandise sells quicker, he thought. The pile on his cart kept growing. He had hopes of making at least forty-five kopecks. But he kept thinking he needed more boughs, so he chopped more and lay the fir branches on the cart.

Finally, the cart was loaded. Antosh inspected it from all sides and was satisfied.

"It'll be enough!" he mumbled aloud and took up the horse's bridle. But after several paces he stopped and looked at his cart again.

But maybe it's not enough, he thought anxiously, so he cut five more boughs and proceeded confidently.

The horse plodded along slowly, step by step. And the slow thoughts in his head kept pace, as if they didn't want to move any faster than the horse. Antosh figured out how much salt, soap, kerosene, and tobacco he would be able to buy with the money earned from the shtetl Jews. Finally, the reckoning exhausted him and he decided that once the few gilden were in hand it would be easier for him to reckon how to spend it. With this decision a heavy weight seemed to fall from him.

When Antosh drove into the shtetl and saw the sukkos already covered with fir boughs, he felt a rent in his heart and he imagined the sukkos and the houses gyrating in the air. But he braced himself with the consoling thought that it was like this every year. Many of the Yids covered their sukkos early on, others much later. That's why it cost more at that time. I'll charge more, he decided, overwhelmed by waves of fear.

He drove on. Two women, one young, the other older, stood on a porch. They pointed at him and giggled until they gasped for breath.

"What are you laughing at?" Antosh asked indignantly.

"Because you brought the fir boughs so early," they said, laughing.

"What do you mean, early?" Antosh couldn't comprehend the laughter.

"Early, early." The women laughed.

"Tfoo!" Antosh spat in a rage and continued driving. Berke himself said in a week, he thought. And I figured it so well: in another two days.

A cold sweat drenched him. Perhaps from the time Berke had spoken to him he'd made a mistake in calculating the days. He realized he must be too late. Of course, all the sukkos were already decked with fir boughs. And Antosh would be left without salt, without tobacco, without soap, without kerosene.

Heartbroken, he drove on with his horse, who seemed to feel his master's great misfortune, and, with his weary head drooping, barely dragged his feet.

Meanwhile, the householders were leaving the synagogue, dressed in their holiday best, carrying their prayer shawls and festival prayerbooks.

Seeing the peasant and his cart laden with fir boughs, the men did not understand at first what was going on and exchanged bewildered looks. Then a pall seemed to come over them: perhaps *they* had erred and brought in Sukkos early.

"What are you bringing?" one of the men asked Antosh.

"What do you mean, what?" Antosh gaped stupidly at them. "I'm bringing fir boughs for Sukkos. Buy them, my dear fellows, buy them," he cried.

The Jews burst into laughter.

"Why do we need fir boughs now, you fool? The festival has already begun," one of the men said to him.

But this great misfortune confused Antosh. He scratched the nape of his neck and yelled, close to tears, · Buy, buy it! I need salt, I need soap, I need kerosene."

The assembled Jews, who at first had laughed at this incident, were now touched. When they saw the poor, thin peasant's despairing face, compassion welled in their hearts.

"A poor goy, it's an awful pity!" said one of the Jews, a pained look on his face.

"Poor man, he hoped to make a fortune with his fir boughs. Now look what happened!" added a second Jew.

"The right thing to do would be to buy his load of fir boughs," suggested another. "It's really a sin not to."

"On the holiday? How?" One of the men rejected the suggestion.

A Jew in the crowd appraised the cart of fir boughs. "The wood alone is worth the money."

"What's the difference what it's worth? It's a holiday."

"No salt, no kerosene, no soap . . ." The peasant sang his refrain, not comprehending what the Jews were saying in Yiddish but sensing that they were favorably disposed to him.

One of the Jews offered a new idea. "Wait! He doesn't need money. He needs goods. Goods without payment can be given on a holiday too."

Everyone became animated. In the circle of Jews stood a shopkeeper whose store was nearby.

"Chaim, give him a couple of pots of salt along with other items he needs. Give him two gilden's worth. It's such a pity. We'll all share the cost."

"Gladly," said Chaim enthusiastically. "A poor goy, it really is a pity."

Chaim called Antosh. With everyone following, he opened the shop and gave the peasant two pots of salt, a piece of soap, a bottle of kerosene, and two packets of tobacco.

Antosh was so overjoyed he didn't know whether to laugh or cry. He was only able to murmur, "Thank you! Thank you!"

And after all the wares were packed, someone suddenly brought him a couple of pieces of challah. "Here. Take it and bring it home."

"And here's more," said another Jew, handing him another chunk.

"And more!"

People were handing Antosh challah from all sides. Confused, he was barely able to utter, "Thank you."

The crowd was pleased and Yankl Leybess, a cheerful man who prepared generously for the holiday and had an intended son-in-law as a guest, brought Antosh a glass of whiskey.

"Here, drink up and have a good trip home."

Antosh quickly downed the whiskey and took a bite of challah.

"I'll never forget this!" he called out gaily.

"You know, he's not a bad goy," said one of the men in the circle.

"You expect him to beat you now?" quipped another Jew with a smile.

The word "beat" cast a pall of gloom over the crowd and they gradually dispersed.

THE TWO
YOUNG BROTHERS

YENKELE AND BERELE, two brothers aged fourteen and
sixteen, studied at the yeshiva in the big city, five miles
from their hometown Dalisovke.

Yenkele was a thin, pale boy with black eyes that peered
out slyly from under his black eyebrows. Berele was taller
and sturdier. His eyes were lighter, his glance more severe
and pensive.

The brothers stayed with a poor relative, a widow who
dealt in secondhand goods and who always came home late
at night. They had no bed but only a wide trunk on which
they slept sweetly, covering themselves with their long
tattered garments. In their dreams they would see their
shtetl, their little street, their home, their father with his
long beard, lightless eyes, and bent back. They would see
their mother with her long, pale, sad face, and they would
hear their little brothers and sisters quarreling, fighting
over a bit of herring. They also dreamt other dreams of
home. When they felt a great tug of homesickness in the
morning, they would run to the Dalisovke Inn to ask the
wagoners if there was a message or letter from home.

The Dalisovke wagoners were good men with tender
hearts and they would surely have felt compassion for the
two poor boys with their glowing eyes who, hearts pounding,
yearned for news from home. But the wagoners were also
very busy. The Dalisovke shopkeepers and merchants had

given them thousands of errands, and even though they carried more mail than the post office, they did it far less efficiently and often misplaced letters and lost parcels. The wagoners would scratch the napes of their necks in a dither and tell everyone, "I'll find it in a minute. Just a moment. No, I don't think I have anything for you."

The two young brothers also stood by, looking longingly and with grieving hearts at Leizer the wagoner, a hairy man who wore a short wadded caftan in summer and winter. The two boys stood and waited, hoping he'd notice them and say something — even a word would do — but Leizer was busy. He went to the yard to feed the horse; he ran into the inn; he had a long talk with the manager of a big warehouse who had brought a load of goods to be sent to a Dalisovke shopkeeper.

The two brothers would stand there until the elder, Berele, would finally lose his patience. Grim-faced and near tears with frustration, he would stammer, "Reb Leizer, do you have a letter from our father?"

But Reb Leizer would either suddenly disappear, run out into the street with someone, or get deeply engaged in a conversation. Berele would wait impatiently for the answer, any answer, that Reb Leizer would finally give over his shoulder, not even looking at the boy.

"There's nothing. Nothing."

"Nothing!" Berele would sigh and gloomily call Yenkele away. Sad and crestfallen, each boy trudged back to the house — their hosts lived on different streets — where the day's meal awaited him.

"He loses the letters, I'm sure!" Yenkele would say a few minutes later.

"He's a nasty man," Berele muttered in agreement.

But one day Leizer the wagoner did give them a short note and a small package.

The letter read:

Dear Children,
Be good and study diligently. We're sending you half a cheese, a quarter of a pound of sugar, and some berry syrup in a jar. Eat it in good health and don't fight.

Your father,
Chaim Hecht

On that day, they thought that Leizer was the nicest man in the world. If they hadn't been ashamed, they would have kissed him and his horse out of love. They wrote an answer at once, guiltily tearing out the opening blank page of the Talmuds they were studying, to use them as stationery, and gave it that evening to Leizer. The wagoner took it with a cold expression on his face, shoved it into his breast pocket, and muttered something that sounded like, "Fine!"

"What did he say, Berl?" asked Yenkele, his heart thumping.

"I think he said, 'Fine!' " Berl answered hesitantly.

"Me too." Yenkele calmed himself. Then he sighed and added anxiously, "He may lose the letter."

"Bite your tongue," Berele said angrily. Absorbed in thought about the fate of their letter, they went to their day's meal.

Three times a week, when Leizer the wagoner arrived in the morning, the two brothers would run to the Dalisovke Inn to ask if a reply had come to their letter, and each time Leizer grew increasingly preoccupied and testy. He answered either with half words, which the two brothers couldn't understand and were afraid to ask him to repeat, or he didn't answer at all, and they left with aching hearts.

But one day the wagoner spoke very clearly and they finally understood him.

"Why are you latching on to me, you rascals? Why are you bothering me? Letter-shmetter. How much did you say you were paying me? Am I your postman, eh? Now run along in good health."

The two young brothers left, but not in good health as he had bade them. Their little hearts were aching terribly, their young, thin legs trembled, and the tears welled up and fell to the ground, trodden by the heavy footfalls of passersby.

After that, they no longer went to Leizer to ask for a letter.

"Let him drop dead," they told each other, even though they didn't really mean it. Secretly they longed just to go see Leizer and his horse and wagon. After all, they came from Dalisovke and that's why the two young brothers loved him.

One Friday during the summer, a couple of weeks after Leizer had chased the brothers away, they sat in the house of their poor relative, talking about home.

"What do you think Father is doing now?" said Yenkele, looking out through the small panes of the little window.

"He must be paring his nails," Berele answered with a sad smile.

"He must be chopping lamb's feet," Yenkele imagined, "and Mama is combing Chaynele's hair and she's probably crying."

"Enough! What nonsense!" Berele stopped him. "How can we know what's going on if we can't see?" And then, to frighten Yenkele, he added, "Perhaps someone's dead."

"Go on with you, you lunatic," Yenkele interrupted him. "If someone dies they send word."

"Perhaps they wrote and the wagoner isn't giving us the letter."

"That's enough now!" Yenkele really became incensed.

"You fool, I'm joking," Berl calmed him. "They're all alive."

Yenkele turned cheerful again and suddenly leapt out of his chair. His eyes sparkling, he shouted, "Berl! Listen to me. Let's mail a letter home."

"Good idea," Berl agreed. "But I don't have any money."

"I have two kopecks left over from the five I got last night," Yenkele said. "The family that invites me for Thursday lunch gives me five kopecks to buy supper, and I have two left over."

"And I have a kopeck too," said Berl. "Just enough for a postcard."

"But who will write it?" asked Yenkele.

"Me," answered Berele. "I'm older and I'm the first-born."

"But I'm giving two kopecks for the card."

"Being a first-born is worth more than two kopecks."

"No. I'll write half and you write half, all right?"

"Fine! Come, let's buy a postcard."

And the two brothers ran to the post office to buy a card.

"There's not going to be any room," Yenkele complained as he contemplated the small postcard on the way home.

"We'll write teeny-tiny letters," Berele suggested.

"Then Father won't be able to read them."

"Never mind. He'll put on glasses."

"Come, let's hurry," Yenkele urged.

His heart was already full of words and he wanted to pour them out onto the bit of paper for which he had expended his entire fortune.

They reached their house and made ready to write.

Berl began, while Yenkele stood and watched.

"Start higher up. There's room for an entire line. Why did you write 'To my dear father' so low down?" Yenkele yelled.

"So where should I put it? In the sky, huh?" asked Berele and pushed Yenkele aside. "Go away! I'll leave you half. Don't disturb me."

"Watch it!"

Yenkele backed off and stared longingly at Berele, who sat there immersed in writing. He wrinkled his brow, dipped his pen, thought awhile, then wrote some more.

"Enough!" Yenkele screamed a few minutes later.

"It's not half a card yet," Berele replied as he continued to write.

"But I should have more than half!" Yenkele said furiously, overwhelmed by the desire to write and pour his heart out to his family back home.

But Berele did not hear. He had begun with fancy Hebrew expressions like "First of all, I want to let you know that I am alive and well," exactly as he had learned from a letter-writing manual, *Letters in Three Languages*. The few words of his own that he had wanted to write were still in his thoughts: He must vilify Leizer the wagoner, tell how many pages of the Talmud he had learned, and ask his parents to send another parcel because they had no invitations to eat on Mondays and Wednesdays and their Tuesday was as good as nothing too.

As Berele continued writing, Yenkele couldn't restrain himself any longer. He noted that Berele was taking up more than half of the card.

He ran to the table, seized the stem of the pen, and shrieked, "Enough!"

"Just three more words," Berele begged.

"All right, but remember! Not a word more!" Yenkele yelled, eyes flashing.

Berele began to write the three words, but the thought he had to express needed ten, fifteen words. And so Berele, writing fervently, pecked away at the paper, and inched into the other half of the card.

"When are you going to stop?" Yenkele screamed and began to cry hysterically, gazing at the small section left for him.

"Wait! I just want to end with 'From your son . . .' " Berl pleaded. "No more than that."

But when Yenkele remembered that he had contributed two entire kopecks for the postcard, yet back home they would read much more of Berele's message, Yenkele made a frenzied attempt to tear the card out of Berl's hand.

"Just let me write 'From your son,' " Berele pleaded more emphatically. "No more than that."

"It'll be fine without it," Yenkele shouted, although he knew deep down that those words should indeed be there. But by now he was seething with rage and he began to pull at the card by force. Berl held on firmly, and Yenkele gave it such a strong tug that the card tore in two.

"What did you do, you idiot?" Berl gaped wildly at Yenkl.

"Just what I wanted!" Yenkele said through choking tears.

"What did you do, you idiot?" Berl asked again, looking dejectedly at the two torn halves of the postcard.

But Yenkele couldn't even answer. The tears gagged him, and out of despair he flung himself against the wall, pulling at his hair. Seeing this, Berl couldn't restrain himself any longer — and the brothers' sobs shook the little house.